DINKY

DAU

Mayhan Bucklers MC Book Four

MariaLisa deMora

Edited by Hot Tree Editing

Proofreading by Whiskey Jack Editing

Copyright © 2021 MariaLisa deMora

First Published 2021

ISBN 13: 978-1-946738-69-1

DEDICATION

Randy Howland

(Tinker)

1948 – 2021

You might have been an asshole to most folks, but I freakin' miss your visits and texts, and yes, even those 3 a.m. drunk and singing phone calls. Covid19 can suck my ass. Thank you for your service.
Ride in paradise, brother.

If anybody can find someone to love them and help them through this difficult thing that we call life, I support that in any shape or form. ~ Will Smith

CONTENTS

ACKNOWLEDGMENTS

Our veterans deserve better. Full stop.

There are so many potential interpertations of that statement, I feel it's important to explain what I mean. Better health care, better pay, better housing, better leaders, better support while transitioning back to civilian life, better protection for LGBTQ+ people in uniform, and better recognition for ALL their service and sacrifices.

The United States isn't alone in this need. I've talked to vets from leading countries around the globe, and every one had a story illustrating how things should be better—but aren't.

Like so many of my stories involving veterans, in *Boocoo Dinky Dau* I've done my best to weave in various real-world details. Information coming to me in the form of quotes, stories of personal experiences, or via views from loved ones.

Boots and Brain are results of all of the above, mixed in with the great individuality these characters brought to their own story.

In this fourth book in the Mayhan Bucklers MC series, we're introduced to a Vietnam vet who has become adept at holding his personal truths close to the vest. Following his service, a long-term friendship developed into a loving same-sex relationship. But he was forced by circumstances to be just as firmly in the small-town closet, even following the loss of his partner years ago.

On the other side of the equation is a sandbox veteran who served through the forced secrecy of Don't Ask, Don't Tell, and carries a profound sense of betrayal paired with shame that the hated policy caused.

Unfortunately, our society hasn't moved on very far from both of these realities. As ever, LGTBQ+ individuals walk daily journeys of public courage, where a single affectionate touch can result in being cast out, or provoke life-threatening reactions from ignorant people. We need a better end to all of those real stories. Because, even as far as we've come, we're not yet at the end of the fight.

Thanks to Becky and Kim with Hot Tree Editing. You folks do good work! Thanks also to Mel with Whiskey Jack Editing for your help with so much of the final polishing. I appreciate alla y'all.

For those who served through DADT: Here's hoping you are forever free.

Woofully yours,
~ML

Boocoo Dinky Dau

The fourth installment in the Mayhan Bucklers MC romance series. A charming tale of love and acceptance in a steamy-sweet May / December MM romance story

Brian "Brain" Nelson has been in the MBMC since Oscar and Kirby recruited him for the resurrected club. Like so many of the members, Brain struggles with demons left from his time in the military. His PTSD and traumatic brain injury symptoms are relentless and plague every aspect of his life with anger, taunting flashes of forgotten moments, and despair.

Clark Donaldson is an old-timer, a member of the original Mayhan Bucklers MC founded by Kirby's and Oscar's grandfather in the aftermath of the brutal Vietnam War. Old Boots has got a thing or two to teach these cherries who want to think they've invented the strain and pain of life after the service.

Brian might be an FNG when it comes to the club, but he's got a lesson or two for Old Boots, too. *Welcome to charm school, old man.*

Chapter One

Brain

Brain's fingers curled tightly around the edges of his mattress, his legs held captive by tangled sheets dampened with sweat. It was dead silent inside his brain, no room for thoughts when the sounds bouncing off the walls were deafening. Flashes lit up the inside of the room, the bombardment incessantly strobing in a disorienting onslaught. Pain ripped behind his eyes, sparking down his spine, arcing across nerve endings raw and scarred from the endless assault. Scents of sand and ozone mixed in confusing fashion with fresh pine and the tinge of woodsmoke.

He blinked, at first not sure he was awake. Brian Nelson, called Brain by his brothers in the Mayhan Bucklers MC, shook his head violently, a hot tear rolling from the corner of one eye. He stared at the window for the hundredth time, verifying the lights were lightning flashes and not streamers from incoming ordnance.

I'm in the clubhouse, not the sandbox.

Sometimes it wasn't easy telling fact from the fiction running on a loop through his head.

Most times.

The headache built, and another blinding flash made him flinch. Rubbing trembling fingers across his forehead, he made a weak effort to soothe the discomfort. Throbbing pain had become his constant companion after the abrupt end to his last tour in the sandbox. The blast that had bounced his brain around inside its hard bone box as it threw him into a wall had also killed two men on his team. Just a normal patrol up to then, as the squad walked streets belonging to a people who hated them. Here he was nearly three years later, and the areas of bruising and bleeding still hadn't completely healed. If he believed the doctors, the injuries that hadn't healed by now probably wouldn't. Those places would atrophy over time, all his symptoms worsening until his body gave up the ghost.

A life sentence of pain gleaned from a moment of inattention. His position that day had been trailing, watching his brothers' backs, staying fifteen meters to the rear of the truck. Instead of remaining focused on the road as he should have been, Brain had found himself paying close attention to the angry faces looking out of upper windows, keeping an eagle eye out for any sign of ambush or attack from above. Through his inattention, he'd closed most of the distance to the slowing truck when it triggered an IED missed by the men leading the column. Nobody's fault but his own. Shit happened every day, and when folks were out to kill you, well, sometimes they succeeded. In his case, their payoff would be just slightly delayed.

The resulting traumatic brain injury and its best friend, PTSD, were his cross to bear. *Alone.* Joining the military had been his choice, and any and all results from that decision were his. As a one-time boyfriend had told him while standing at Brain's hospital bedside during his single, very short visit, there had been no sense sentencing them both to a slow death.

Like it would have killed Erwin to stick around. Drama king.

That was not long after the ending of Don't Ask, Don't Tell, when it had been hard to trust that being queer and ignoring DADT protocol wouldn't still get a person booted to the curb with limited veteran benefits if they earned a less-than-honorable discharge. All around him, he'd seen how being closeted was still strongly encouraged, especially for soldiers who considered themselves lifers. Erwin had been out and proud, and Brain had known the only reason they'd lasted months through the relationship was that he'd been deployed when they were only a few weeks in. Erwin did long distance very well, and the enthusiasm of his video calls had fooled Brain into believing it was more. He sure hadn't expected to be dumped like a bag of trash, but c'est la vie.

Stateside and newly single, he'd allowed Uncle Sam to deal with the physical fallout from the injuries. Being passed around from rehab to rehab was easier than trying to sort shit on his own as the docs worked on the various deficits, but it meant adapting to new situations every few months—something that was exhausting by itself. That decision had turned out to be a seriously lucky break when Brain had met one of the founders of the newly resurrected Mayhan Bucklers MC during one of those therapy stays. He'd clicked with Kirby Westbrook immediately and found the same camaraderie with Kirby's cousin, Oscar Mayhan, the other founder. The proposed brand-new foundation seemed tailor-made for him, and Brain had jumped at the chance to be one of the first new members.

The club was based in bumfuck Texas, but whatever. Wasn't like he'd be around long anyway, not with his prognosis. Years at best, but decades weren't in the cards for him.

Good thing he'd learned early and well how to keep his mouth shut and zippers up in the service, because the club had become another version of DADT for him. Hot as some of the guys were, each of his brothers in the club was straight as the proverbial arrow. Knowing that fact, it was reasonably easy to hide in plain sight. He couldn't see them accepting a gay man in their vicinity, and he was okay with that. The benefits found by working through his emotional and physical issues in a supportive group like the club far outweighed any arguments against.

That avoidance applied to new members and old, because the original club had its roots in the Vietnam era. Club lore had the brotherhood breathed to life by Kirby's and Oscar's grandfather right here in Mayhan, Texas, standing shoulder to shoulder with three staunch friends and a group of like-minded veterans. This far down the line from that point of origin, only a few of the original members were left alive. The other OGs were all gone on ahead, riding in paradise.

Brain smiled, fingers still rubbing gently across his forehead. Clark Donaldson, renamed Old Boots by Brain, was one of those OGs. He'd lived a hell of a life, and for a man in his sixties was fit and full of energy. *More than me, some days.*

Fit? Hell yeah, Old Boots was fit. Broad shoulders, lean hips, a rigid bearing branded into him from his time standing at attention through monsoons and heat waves. Sky blue eyes danced with good nature, regardless of whether Brain was having a decent or bad day. Boots'ss bright smile exposed not only his sense of humor but also a crooked eyetooth that Brain found endearing.

Fit, and way fuckin' straight. Brain sighed. *About my kinda luck, ain't it just? Mooning over this gorgeous older man, and it's got to be one that don't bat for my team.*

Brilliance flared outside, followed by a window-rattling boom that ran any thoughts from his mind. Brian rolled off the mattress, landing flat on the floor. He wiggled sideways until he was underneath his bunk and waited.

White light blinked into and out of existence around the bed, kept from touching him by the frame above him. He held his breath and counted silently, lips moving as he kept track—three seconds until the detonation sounded.

That one was close. Any closer, and they'd be hitting the barracks next. For all the noise of the sound waves after the bombs hit, the continuing bombardment was eerily silent. No incoming screeches telegraphed proximity. That sound was always terrifying in the way it got louder and louder until a body would think if they looked up, they'd see the charge coming in hot wearing an image of themselves. *Dead-set targeted.* He wove his fingers around the exposed wooden slats supporting the bunk above him, putting enough tension through his arms it would take a close blast to blow it off.

The sound of rain came suddenly, loud and deafening. Brian heard the tattoo of sleet or small hail blasting against the glass in the window. He craned his neck to get a glimpse of it around the bedframe.

Why is there a window in the barracks?

That just didn't make sense. Windows were fragile, useless things, more likely to be used as a weapon than protection.

Since when does it rain in the sandbox?

"Brain?"

He froze and then flexed his biceps, pulling hard enough on the pieces of wood that they creaked overhead.

None of this makes a lick of sense.

No one in the platoon called him anything but Nelson. Their Looey didn't like nicknames, so he'd strongly recommended the troops keep to surnames instead. Brain was...

Not yet.

"You under there, buddy?"

The voice was familiar. Made Brian think about the fuzzy blue blanket he'd had years ago. Every time he'd been sick, his mom would bring it and wrap the comforting warmth around him tightly. The blanket was just the color of the sky in summer, light and bright blue.

The prettiest color in the world.

"Noisy outside tonight, thought I'd come check on ya."

Blood flooded to his groin, and Brian suddenly remembered the first time he'd gotten an inconvenient boner, the moment when his world had tipped up on edge for an instant, threatening to topple him into a dark crevasse.

He'd grown up thin and small. That meant in seventh and eighth grades, his sports options were limited to weight-class one-on-one competitions or individual events. Wrestling? *Oh, hell no.* Just the idea of putting on the singlet and standing in the middle of a building full of shouting people had his stomach standing on end, so that was out.

Track is where it's at. A near cousin to that saying had been their track and field coach's motto. Wiry and strong were the right combination for a runner, and when a body added in the kind of determination Brian had been blessed with, it was the icing on the cake.

"I'm just gonna sit here with you for a while, until you feel like you can come out from under there."

The boner.

That had happened during practice his freshman year. High school had meant moving campuses, a whole new minefield of potential friends and enemies. Kids came from different neighborhoods and socioeconomic groups, providing greater diversity in the entirety of the student body. So many new chances for crippling social failure.

Tryouts for the track team had gone well for Brian, and he'd quickly secured his favorite events, long distance and cross-country. There'd been a half a dozen other boys who'd qualified for the same events, and training with the others had helped make Brian an even better competitor.

What about the boner?

Typically, their early morning sprints naturally moved into a mile-long training run, with a preassigned pace. Jonathon Newman was Brian's main competition for their team's top spot in their events. One day, by the half-mile mark in their run, Jonny had gotten a couple of quick strides ahead. Then Brian had noticed how the muscles in Jonny's back flexed with each pump of his arms, how the high globes of his ass bunched and stretched with every stride, moving sinuously underneath the thin nylon practice shorts.

That's when the boner happened. His wiener had been bent to the side, trapped in place and painful as it filled with blood, chubbing up while he watched another boy's ass get farther and farther ahead of him. He'd ended the mile walking, doing complex math problems in his head to lose the stiffy. Brian had to lie to the coach about shin splints, then endure hours of ice therapy as a tortured result.

Brian remembered thinking, "I can't be gay. My dad'll kill me."

"What's that, buddy?"

Brian blinked and stiffened, twisting fingers gone lax into tight fists around the wooden slats above him.

The tracers from incoming rounds lit up the room again, and he flipped to his side, curling into a ball with his hands laced over the back of his head, elbows bent up beside his ears to protect against the blast of noise he expected.

Nelson waited for it to be over.

Chapter Two
Old Boots

Over the cacophony of an East Texas summertime thunderstorm, Clark heard Brain shift underneath the bed, the man's prayers for grace and safety scarcely a murmur. The storm was beginning to move along, headed east towards Shreveport and the states beyond. Clark knew from experience it would be a couple of hours yet before he'd be able to get Brain out from under the bed and back into it.

In the lull between rumbles of thunder, he caught the creak of a board in the hallway and looked up to see the door swinging silently open. Kirby Westbrook stood in the opening, the hand not on the doorknob scrubbing across his jaw. Undoubtedly he'd climbed out of bed with his fiancée, Dana, to come check on Brain. *Because that's the kind of men Dall raised.* Kirby was a grandson of Clark's long-time friend and mentor, Randall Mayhan, the original founder of the MBMC. Dall—or Pops, as everyone else had called him—had another grandson also involved with the club, Oscar Mayhan.

It felt like a slap in the face the first time Kirby had come home to explain to the few surviving MBMC members what he'd wanted to do with the club. Not that they'd ever been outlaw. Clark stifled a snort at the very idea. Dall wouldn't have stood for that kind of muckin' about, not a chance. But taking a respected motorcycle club with its roots in a quiet protest against unjust wars and turning it into a foundation to support wounded veterans seemed a long stretch. Clark had been glad to see his fears were unfounded, as Kirby proceeded to transform all those raggedy dreams into reality. The boy had breathed life and excitement into the club, and now Clark could honestly say he'd never been as thrilled as when Kirby asked him a few months ago to take over Oscar's old spot as in-house crowd control.

"You got him?" Kirby's grumbled question fell in between peals of thunder, his gaze going to the window and then back to Clark.

From his position on the floor, back leaning against the wall, Clark told Kirby, "Yeah, I got him. Storm came up fast. Caught me off guard." He shuffled his outstretched legs, recrossing his ankles as he pinched the fabric of his pajama bottoms and tugged, so they didn't twist, then straightened the long sleeves of his top, pulling the hems down over his tattooed arms. "Won't happen again, Kirby. I'm gonna find an app that'll help me sort it better." He knew the way he said "app" was weird but didn't care. When you didn't grow up with technology, being able to use it at all should be impressive, much less using it to figure out how to make lives easier.

"Okay, I'm going back to bed. Come get me if you need me, old man." Kirby took a step closer and held out his fist, and Clark met it with his own knuckles, giving him a gentle pound.

"Pretty sure I can take care of one boy by myself. Fuck you and that old man shit." He lifted his other hand, phone already poised in his grip. "Go away. I've got porn to watch."

"Jesus. I don't wanna know." The door clicked as it closed, and Clark listened to the footsteps fading away as he grinned.

"Amateur." Opening the app store, Clark started browsing for something that would give him enough warning to get out ahead of whatever next set of storms would inevitably come their way. "Brain, how you doing under there, buddy?" He didn't expect an answer and wasn't upset when nothing was directed at him, all of Brain's mutterings addressed towards a deity of his youth. "Gonna make life easier for both of us going forwards."

His third search in the store returned mixed results, and he was annoyedly flipping to yet another page of icons that had nothing to do with warning him about the weather when he caught sight of an app that didn't quite belong.

"Hello, what do we have here?" The image of an isolated male chest with fur and leather harness was intriguing. "Let us peruse the wares, shall we, Brain?" The extra images included in the app profile were hard body parts in isolation, no faces, and no peen. "Dammit, Scotty, we need more powah." He tapped the download link, then went back to his search. The next page presented an app for parents of special needs children. From the description, it looked picture-perfect for his requirements—intensity alarms based on the local radar, not fed via a weather system centered in another state. As good as their tools were, here in Northeast Texas, storms could wax and wane within an hour or two, and being able to predict things like the thunder factor instead of just precipitation would make a difference for Brain. "Found us something. Now to see how well it works. You doin' okay under there, Brain?"

"Yeah." Hoarse, rough as if he'd gone days in the sandbox without water, Brain answered him.

"Alrighty. I'm just gonna hang out here for a bit. Got some apps to download, see what they have in store for us." He shifted, recrossing his ankles and moving weight to his other ass cheek. "Should have brought a pillow in here to sit on." Movement underneath the bed snagged his attention, and he watched from the corner of his eye as Brain dragged himself closer to the edge, hand over hand, using the wooden slats above him for leverage. "I'm not goin' anywhere, Brain. Take your time."

"I'm okay." The three-syllable lie was smoother than the previous grunted single word, and Clark rolled his eyes, going through the preferences and settings on the weather app. "What, old man? I am."

"Again, I'm not goin' anywhere in a hurry, so you don't have to bullshit me." The phone vibrating silently in his hand was gratifying, and he smiled down at the device. The alert showed thunder could be expected for the next ten minutes, and a quick glance out the window revealed that to be on target. Scrolling ahead to the forecast, he frowned. According to this app, over the next five hours or so, a series of remaining energy waves could easily turn into the same kind of pop-up storms, until the heat from the day disappeared entirely.

"What's wrong, Old Boots?"

Clark smoothed out his frown before glancing over at Brain. *God, the man is gorgeous.* Tousled hair swooping over his high forehead, Brain had his head resting on his toned and flexed bicep, and those dark eyes were half hooded, staring at Clark with such intensity he felt bare. Not naked, and he ignored the way his dick twitched at that idea, but as if with a single look, Brain had stripped away all his defenses and saw him, the man he'd been hiding for decades. *Shiiit.*

"Where are your meds, bud?" Clark flashed the screen at the man, then angled it away. The tease wouldn't be enough to pull him out from under the bed, but it might be a start. "There're more storms coming, and we both need to get ready."

"I can handle it." Anger flooded Brain's face, and his mouth turned down in a scowl. "You think I can't handle a little wind and rain?"

"You and I both know that's not the issue, so don't insult the two of us like that. This first storm triggered you, and you're gonna be exhausted going into the next one tonight. Not a good recipe, Brain." He made a come-on gesture with two fingers, curling them over his palm. "Come on out if you can, and let's get ready."

"I fucking hate that I need a babysitter." Brain's gaze danced around the room, not landing on anything for more than a second, including Clark's face. "You don't know how it feels."

Dall stared at Clark, any anger he felt well buried behind what looked like compassion and a tiny bit of fear. "I'm not babysitting you, asshole. I'm tryin' to keep you out of the nuthouse. Last time you went off on a bender, you tore up the front of the mayor's house, ripped all his wife's flowers out of the ground. You remember waking up in the holding cell, convinced the Cong had you again? You'd been looking for tunnels, you said, because the mayor had looked at you funny. Jesus, Clark, I'm tryin' to help you here, brother."

Clark dropped his head to stare down at the phone. He blinked hard and fast, and gradually, the screen came back into focus, memories put where they belonged—in the past. "I know I can't understand everything, Brain. But you might be surprised at what I do." Shoving away from the wall, he pushed to his good knee, then his feet with a groan, his low back complaining about the position he'd occupied for the past few hours. An old injury that never quite got the message it was time to shut up. "Get your damned meds, Brain. I'm getting a fucking chair. I'm too old to be campin' out on the floor."

"Nobody asked you to." Brain slid out from underneath the bed and stood in a single fluid movement. He was strong, the toned muscles in his abdomen and chest bunching underneath his skin. His skintight briefs did nothing to hide the bulge at his groin, and without a doubt, the man was packing. Clark sucked his tongue back into his mouth. The damn thing had been trying to escape and swipe a fat strip across his bottom lip.

Jesus, I'm tired.

"I'll be back in a minute." His bare feet shuffling across the cool, smooth boards, Clark slipped out the door and into the hallway, pausing to get his dick back under control.

No idea why that boy does it for me, but damn me to hell and back, he does.

Chapter Three
Brain

Watching Old Boots stalk out of his room made Brain's stomach churn. *Why did it have to be him tonight?* For all his protestations, he well understood his brothers' desire to ensure his safety. There'd been enough episodes where he'd been out of control in a way that frightened him later, and he knew it had to be unsettling to watch. So sure, maybe he did need a babysitter, someone to ensure he didn't hurt anyone else—*or myself*—but why did it have to be the one man who made him *want* again.

No way I'm flyin' around my own flagpole, he reminded himself.

Even without it being stated plainly, he couldn't put aside his belief that coming out would be a quick uninvite to the club, and this—the group of men and the support they provided—was something he needed. Sex wasn't. Plus, if he got too strong an urge, Texarkana was just a short run up the highway. He'd found two different bars over there that no one in Mayhan would be caught dead in, so as long as he restricted himself to nameless encounters there, he could get by. *I will get by.*

The door creaked, startling him, and he realized he hadn't moved an inch since Old Boots had left.

How long have I been standing here, droolin' over the man?

"Shit," he muttered, quickly sitting on the edge of the bed to hide his growing erection. Reaching out for the nightstand drawer, he glanced up to see Old Boots wrestling with an armchair he'd apparently retrieved from the main floor. *Dammit, the man's gonna hurt his back worse than it already is.*

"Hell, Boots, let me help you." Springing up, he grabbed the edge of the door and swung it wide as he took hold of one side of the chair. Between them, they angled it through the opening, and Boots gestured towards a corner with a lift of his chin and a grunt. "Got it."

The chair's legs settled silently on the floor, and Brain looked up to find Boots'ss gaze angled down. Brain's underwear had no chance to hide the rigid state of his lingering erection.

"Shit," he said again, covering his dick with one hand. "Sorry."

Turning away, he stalked towards the window. There he paused next to the glass-paned view of the outside world, trying to think of anything but the man in the room with him. *Boring as hell baseball, dogs taking a shit, old church ladies. Anything.*

"You take your meds yet?"

Brain let out a silent sigh of relief that Boots was willing to ignore the elephant in the room, then had to stifle a snort at the idea of him being the elephant. "Not yet," he admitted. "My head's fuzzy. I didn't forget or anything. I just didn't get there yet."

"It's all right. I brought you some water. Why don't you come do it now?" Rustling sounds behind him were revealed by the window's reflection to be Boots moving things around on his nightstand. "Where do you keep them?" The slide of wood on wood was the nightstand drawer, and Brain had only an instant to wonder why the sound was terrifying when Boots took in a sharp, sudden breath, and he remembered. "Here they are." In the wavery reflection, the old man's hand reached into the drawer and returned with a pill bottle in hand, and then that same wood-on-wood slide was him closing it.

There was no way the old man hadn't seen his dildo, clean and resting on a cloth, tube of lube nestled right next to it for ease of access.

Shit.

The pill bottle rattled as Brain turned around, fixedly staring at Boots as the man shook two tablets into the palm of his hand. "I—uh—"

"Come on, Brain. I don't bite."

What if I want you to bite me?

Brain shushed the unhelpful voice in his head and reached out, taking Boots's offer like the lifeline it was.

Maybe they'd never have to discuss any of this. He could tell Kirby he wasn't comfortable with Boots watching over him, and Kirby'd bend over backwards to change things. The man was all about making his brothers' lives better, and Brain knew he could use that to cover up all the things that had happened tonight.

The pills dropped into his palm, and a bottle of water was thrust in his direction. He tossed the meds to the back of his throat, swallowing them dry as he accepted the water, careful to keep his fingers from brushing against the other man's. A twist of the cap, and he turned it up, chasing the scratch of the pills with cold liquid that tasted like ambrosia. He stopped himself after downing half the bottle and looked up to see Boots smiling at him, a surprising fondness in his expression.

"Thanks" was all Brain could say. He recapped the bottle and placed it on a folded piece of paper towel that had appeared on the nightstand, next to another water bottle.

"That one's yours too," Boots said, his voice having taken on a low, sexy growl. "I brought it for you." Brain glanced at him, then back to the nightstand, where his no-longer-secret desires hid. "It's all good, Brain. I got you, brother."

Brother. That single word hammered home why he shouldn't perv on the men who shared this house with him.

Oh yeah. Need to hit up Texarkana soon.

"I hate you have to spend your time like this, old man." Brain returned to the window, staring out as he ignored the movement behind him. "Not like my head's going to be suddenly fixed tomorrow. I'm just fuckin' broken."

"Nah, you're not broken, Brain. Bent maybe, but not broke. And there's not a thing you can do or say that would shock or surprise me." Boots's voice dipped lower, and Brain turned to look at him. Gaze directed at the floor, the older man felt behind him for the arms of the chair and dropped heavily into the seat once he had his hands in place to support his descent. "Trust me, you boys aren't the first to come home from war with damage."

Brain studied Boots, slowly picking apart the statement and matching it with what he knew about the man. "You were in Vietnam." That statement earned him a hot glance from underneath Boots's brows, but no response. "You don't talk about it."

"What's there to say? It all happened a long, long time ago." Boots sighed and stretched back into the chair, legs extended and his elegant feet pointing and flexing. "Matters little anymore, the way the world's going these days."

Brain settled on the edge of the bed nearest the pillows, far away from where Boots sat. "How old were you when you were drafted?"

Boots's laughter was surprising, light and airy, full of good humor. A direct contrast from the man's dark gaze a few moments ago. "I wasn't drafted. I volunteered." The expression on his face was brightly amused. "More fool was I, but too young to know better."

"How old were you? They didn't take anyone under eighteen, right?" Brain shook his head. "I mean, I can't judge you for volunteering, not when I did the same."

"Young enough my momma had to sign for me. Lied for me, too." Boots smiled, the corners of his mouth curling softly. "Fifteen was my bulletproof phase, I guess."

"Fifteen? How the hell would the government even allow that?" *Jesus.* When Brain had been that age any attempt at carrying a fully loaded pack would have put him on his ass. *Motherfuckers.* After his experience with DADT, it shouldn't have been a surprise that as long as they lied prettily enough, back then Uncle Sam would have been happier loading up on 15-year-olds than they were now with men like him.

"They didn't, but they sure didn't ask any questions when I walked in with my momma at my heels. Military forces were struggling with the draft. Enough men who didn't want to serve were presenting with 4-F paperwork or heading up to Canada, so the recruitment officers didn't ask twice if my mom was sure. They never asked me anything. Just had me raise my hand to swear." Boots's gaze turned inward, and his full lips thinned, pressing tightly together. "Stupid is as stupid does, I guess. I turned sixteen on a plane headed to Vietnam in '70."

"Jesus." Brain tried to think of what he'd been doing at sixteen and could only come up with those fucking high school memories. *The boner.* "I can't imagine what that'd be like."

"Like it was literal hell. But by the time I realized what an idiot I was, we were deep in-country. Had an officer try to take me under his wing, wanted me to do back-of-base duties to keep me safe, and all I wanted was to prove my mettle was as stout as that of any other man. Marine jarhead, through and through. Oorah." He shook his head, gaze bouncing up to meet Brain's, then darting away. "If I knew then what I know now, life'd be different, but ain't that the usual cry of old men?"

"You're not that old. Fit as fuck too." The words were out of his mouth before he could stop them, and he hoped Boots would chalk it up to the meds talking. "I mean, not that I'm lookin'." *Shit, just dig that hole a little deeper, why don't you?* "Y-Y-You know what I mean." When he pried his gaze from the wall behind Boots and glanced at his face, the man was sporting hot color high in his cheeks.

"You're a shithead, Brain." Boots propped a heel against the foot of the bed, the view of his bare sole and ankle somehow intimate. *I'm so fucked.* "No idea why I like your ass, but I do."

Don't say it. Don't say it. "Why you lookin' at my ass, Boots?" He wiggled farther down in the bed, head propped up on a hand, elbow buried in the pillow. "Don't answer that. Do not answer that." Brain giggled. "Oh, shit. I'm fuckin' stoned."

"Yeah, you are." Boots smiled, lips parting to give Brain a glimpse of that damn crooked tooth. "No worries, man. It's all good." Boots looked down at his lap and picked up his phone as the smile fell away, a frown taking its place. "Weather's about ten minutes out, probably start picking up lightning any time now."

"It's okay, Boots. I'm good with you in here." Brain felt pleasantly loose and relaxed, a thousand miles away from where he'd been half an hour ago. "Shoulda taken the pills when I went to bed. We'd both be sleepin'."

"Yeah, but then I'd miss this scintillating conversation." Boots fiddled with his phone some more, and Brain watched as those two red patches appeared in his cheeks again. "Among other things."

Brain didn't respond, just oozed down into the bed, head resting on the pillow now. A low rumble filled the air, and he saw Boots's gaze flick to the window, then to him. "I'm good, Boots. I'm good, swear. Pills do more than take the edge off. Don't tell Dominic, but they're a good tool to have, even if I hate how they make me feel." He swallowed hard. "Thirsty."

Boots smiled at him again, that soft and concerned expression back as his feet dropped from the foot of the bed. The older man eased closer and picked up the half-empty bottle. The lid was tight, and Boots had to lay his phone on the nightstand to use both hands.

Brain reached out without thinking and snagged the device, ignoring the hissed, "Brain, no."

Lifting the screen up, he stared at...an erect dick, male hand curled possessively around the root, heavy balls appearing below. He touched the screen, and the image changed to one of a broad chest with tufts of hair between the pecs and around the nipples. He tapped once more, and the image changed again, a down-angled shot of a high, round ass, thick fingers clamped around each cheek in a proud spread showing a dark shadow in the cleft.

The phone was plucked from his fingers, and he scrabbled for it, wanting those images back because, *damn*, every one of those did it for him. Then he looked up into Boots's face. The expression of absolute panic on the man's face registered and then was ignored as Brain realized what he'd done, what his rapidly filling cock was doing to him, because of course Boots couldn't miss that little fact. *Shit, how the hell do I fix this without completely outing myself?*

"Where's that weather app?" Yes, that's what his mind decided to go with, deflection having worked wonders in the past. Now, if only Boots would be willing to go along with him. Brain held his breath, releasing it slowly when he saw how red Boots's face was.

"Oh, it's here."

Boots dicked around with the phone, then handed it back to Brain as if nothing had happened, as if he had nothing to hide. *Maybe he doesn't?* Brain tried to weigh the odds of his fucked-up head making up the whole thing, not happy with the chances. He accepted the phone, and sure enough, a band of storms looked to be closing in on a pulsing red dot in the center of the screen that he assumed indicated their location.

"Looks bad." He offered the phone up, then took the opened bottle from Boots and drained it. "With the meds, I'm sure I'll be okay if you want to head out. I'm dosed up and ready for anything."

"I'll stick tight if it's all the same to you." Boots turned, and Brain reached out, snagging his hand on the man's elbow. Boots looked back, one brow lifted in a question.

"I—can you stay here?" Brain patted the bed next to himself. "Show me the radar? Maybe if I see it coming, it'll be easier?"

Boots stared at him, and Brain would have given anything to know what was going on in the man's head.

Finally, after blowing out a hard breath, the man nodded. "Sure, Brain. I can do that."

Brain shuffled to the side, pulling one of the pillows with him.

"Chair wasn't much better than the floor anyway. Maybe this'll wreck my back less." Boots took the other pillow, propped it against the headboard, and then angled himself onto the mattress with a groan. Heat from his body filled the space between them immediately, and Brain watched as the man stretched out his legs, primly straightening his pajamas before crossing one ankle over the other. "Few more minutes," he said, holding the screen where Brain could watch it too. Another peal of thunder sounded outside, low and rumbling. "Tell me if you need anything."

"I will." Brain bunched up his pillow and shoved it underneath his head. "This helps."

"I'll do whatever you need, brother."

"Tell me about your time in-country." Brain kept his eyes on the screen, watching as the line of storms crept closer. "When did you get home?"

"I did two thirteen-month tours, back-to-back, no home time to speak of. Always felt like I flew in one minute and out the next. Hot? Hell, I never knew it could get that hot. I'd always thought Texas had a lock on the heat. Then I spent my first summer in the jungle and never complained about Texas heat again." Boots's hand trembled. The shaking stilled when he propped his wrist against his thigh. "Vietnam was the birth and death knell for my service. Longest years of my life right there, I tell you what."

"I was 2001 to 2014. All over the sandbox, then had my finale in Afghanistan. The Taliban were the enemy back then." Brain scoffed. "Hell, they're probably still the enemy, I don't know. I had another two years on my ticket when I got my brain scrambled." He stared up at the ceiling, watching as flashes of light played across the acoustic tiles. "Been bouncin' around since then. Luck had me trying yet another therapy plan, which fortunately for me intersected the same time and treatment as Kirby." He yawned, scooching closer to the source of the heat next to him. "Got me here, so I shouldn't complain."

"You're allowed to complain all you want, soldier." The deep voice vibrated the air around him more than the thunder did, and he laughed at the idea. "Why don't you sleep, Brain? You could use the shut-eye."

"Will you stay with me?" God, he hated his weak, needy whine. *Too fuckin' soft.*

"Of course I will, brother. Course I will. Sleep." His pillow moved, and Brain's eyes opened to see Boots's hands first unbunching the pillow, then smoothing it out underneath Brain's cheek. "I'm right here. Gonna catch some rack time myself. Win-win for both of us."

"Okay, then." Darkness descended with his eyelids, and Brain found himself focusing on the sound of Boots's breathing instead of the thunder, the steady cadence settling his nerves in a way he didn't mind one bit.

Chapter Four
Old Boots

Wakefulness came slowly, and Clark looped his arm around the waist of the hard body snuggled against him, pulling it closer. He groaned and stretched his legs before tucking them into the natural curve of the man's bent knees. It had been years since he'd fallen asleep with another man, and damn if he hadn't missed it. *Not since Dall and I*—he shoved the idea aside. Hookups were great, but who wanted to spend time and brain cells on someone who could dick really well but couldn't put two sentences together?

"How you doin'?" He asked the question with his lips pressed tight to the nape in front of him, nose buried in the short auburn hair as he racked his mind for clues as to the man's identity.

"I'm good, Boots." Brain's voice was like a shock of cold water, and Clark shoved himself backwards, separating from the man in an instant. "Aww, why'd you have to go and do that? You're warm." Brain's booty scooted backwards, tucking against Clark's groin in a way that had his dick waking up to say hello. A hand appeared over Brain's shoulder, open, waiting, and he tentatively placed his palm in the warm grip. Two tugs had him closer, chest pressed against Brain's back as his arm was pulled around and under Brain's arm, palm flat over the center of the man's chest. "So warm."

It was dark outside, the storms having moved off while he slept, so he had no idea of how late it might be. *Brain is probably still woozy from the drugs.* That made the most sense. The idea of Brain—his mind shorted out at the thought. It didn't matter Brain had a good-sized dildo in his drawer. Liking prostate stimulation didn't automatically equate to gay. *Man has me being in his bed confused with me keeping him safe. That's all it is.* Brain's breathing changed to a slower cadence that included a tiny whistle on each exhale. Clark let out a quiet, relieved gust of air and slowly extricated himself from the covers. Carefully rolling out of bed, he left Brain grumbling in his sleep, endearingly smacking his lips.

Clark didn't know how he'd gone from sitting against the headboard to being flat-out on the bed next to Brain, covers to his waist, but he knew it couldn't happen again. A quick check of the weather app showed it had been nearly two hours, and as expected, the cooler nighttime air aloft had lost the ability to support the development of more storms.

Clark slipped into the hallway and pulled the door shut behind him before shuffling downstairs to where his bedroom waited. In an uneasy truce with nature's brutal progression, he'd accepted Kirby renovating what had once been a second treatment room into a suite for him. The change kept Clark from having to go up and down the stairs more often than necessary for his back. Lately, Brain had been the only thing that had him traveling to the second floor. *Getting old sucks,* he told himself as he pushed open the door, seeing his own covers thrown back, left that way when he'd unassed with haste after the first blast of thunder had woken him.

"Shit like that can't happen again." He sighed and thumbed the latch on the doorknob. It was a nod towards privacy, something easily defeated by just a paperclip, but anyone trying to turn it and encountering resistance would at least call out before they entered. "I've made it this long without fucking myself over. I should be able to manage going forward."

Stepping past the bed, he leaned into the bathroom and turned on the shower, pulling the curtain mostly closed to keep the overspray to a minimum. He stripped with efficient movements, boxers and pj's tossed into the hamper as his dick bounced and bounded between his legs, obstinately rigid. Pushing past the curtain, he arranged it behind him with one hand as he picked up his bottle of all-in-one shampoo and bodywash. A tiny puddle in the palm of one hand, and he slicked it along his shaft, working up a fistful of suds in no time.

Clark tried to focus on the images from the hookup app he'd looked at. Calling up memories of cocks and holes, and pretty boys with cum streaked across their chests and faces. Still, his stubborn mind insisted on circling back to the feel of holding a man in his arms, of how kissing Brain's neck had been intimate and special, the way the man's ass had cradled his hard cock, and the erotic sounds Brain had made as he nestled into Clark's big spoon, as if he'd found something he liked. Then he remembered the way Brain's dick had hardened at the images on the phone, tenting his briefs in an unmistakable reaction that Clark had immediately decided to ignore.

Clark granted himself one-time permission to explore what might have been—instead of picturing anonymous images, he concentrated on the noises Brain would make as Clark worked him open. The way Brain would clamp down on fingers spearing and curving inside him, brushing against the spongy gland that would make him speak to God. Brain's face looking up at him, eyes half-hooded and mouth open in an endless gasp as Clark pushed inside for the first time, strong hands sliding up his arms and shoulders, down his back to cup his ass and pull him deeper.

He grunted, hand moving to twist around the head of his dick, wringing every last ounce out of his orgasm, splattering his hand and wrist with the hot, white fluid that disappeared immediately, sucked down the drain along with the suds.

Clark leaned one forearm against the shower wall, letting the hot water run through his hair and down the back of his neck.

"Shit." He shouldn't have done that. Guilt and shame crept in that he'd used a friend—*a brother*—in such a way. Not that it hadn't happened before, but that time was long in the past and had wound up with a much nicer ending than he expected this time.

I just can't let it happen again.

He turned off the water and grabbed a towel, then scrubbed at himself roughly.

The memory of Brain arching backwards against him rocketed through his head, and he closed his eyes.

"I'm so fucked."

Chapter Five
Brain

Pulling in a deep breath, Brain stretched out in his bed, uncurling from the position he'd apparently occupied all night, if his complaining muscles were to be believed. Moving cautiously, he angled his neck, waiting for the usual pain in his head to sit up and smack him down. It didn't. He tried a different stretch, one that released a series of groan-inducing pops all along his spine. *Jesus.* He couldn't remember the last time he'd felt like this, and he briefly contemplated just staying in bed all day in case it could last. After a couple of yawns also failed to produce pain, he opened his eyes and took in the light flooding the room.

It had to be midmorning at least. His stomach growled and churned, making him grin. *Maybe even after lunch.* His head never let him sleep in, the pain waking him like clockwork every couple of hours throughout the night.

Brain knew the interrupted rest was a factor in what had become a daily escalation of his pain, but he hadn't figured out how to ignore the demands of his own body.

"Awwhhh," he yawned again, eyes watering. *What the hell happened to me last night?*

He'd lost time; he knew that. Exiting from underneath his bed and finding Boots there was a sure giveaway that he'd had a flashback. Last night seemed like more, though, and he wished he could remember.

Easing his legs over the edge of the mattress, Brain gingerly levered himself to a sitting position, ready and willing to resume the previous prone one if the pain in his head attacked, but it stayed at bay. Not even at bay. There was no niggling tension in his neck or scalp that presaged an imminent headache, and he reveled in the idea that maybe today could be pain free.

His gaze fell on the pillows arranged at the head of the bed, and he froze. His pillow was crunched and wrinkled, as it ordinarily was after a rough night. That wasn't concerning, not at all, but the state of the second pillow had all his attention. It, too, was wrinkled, the center depressed as if someone had slept beside him. Before he could stop himself, he bent close and inhaled. The scent of a familiar soap filled his nose.

Boots slept with me. Reflexively shaking his head, he paused midmotion and waited, sighing with relief when it failed to awaken his typical headache. *Boots didn't sleep with me. He probably just needed to stretch out a minute*

35

after sitting on the floor all night. That made more sense, and Brain huffed out a soft laugh before picking up the pillow and inhaling again. *So shoot me if my head's dreaming for more.* He imagined hard arms around him, holding him close, Boots's voice in his ear as he talked him into resting.

Something he did remember was being handed his meds, which normally didn't work if he was already in the midst of a flashback or panic attack. That was after he'd helped Boots with the chair now looming in the corner. *That's not it.* Something else had happened to help him center himself enough to sleep. *So what if he did climb into bed with me? It doesn't mean anything.* Boots would do anything for the members of the MBMC, and that included him.

Feet on the floor, he stood, then lurched forwards, a hand to the wall in front of him as the room spun. "Shit." Eyes open, he fixed his gaze at a point on the wall, knowing from extensive experience that closing them would only intensify the vertigo. "Shit, fuck."

"Brain? You okay?" The door opened, and Boots walked into the room and straight to where Brain stood. He wavered, and Boots's arms were there to steady him, holding him upright, surrounding him with strength and that damned scent that left him breathless on top of being dizzy. "Hold on, Brain. I got you."

Gaze still fixed on that same spot, he tilted his head to the side, resting it against Boots's shoulder, and took a deep breath. "Just dizzy," he explained, leaning more heavily on the man next to him. "Thanks, Boots."

"It's all good." Boots turned him so Brain stood chest to chest. "I was comin' up to check on you. Last time I looked in, you were still sleeping. How do you feel except for the dizziness?"

"Good." He took a breath as the room settled around him. "No headache for a change, which is a fuckin' miracle. I just stood up too fast, is all." Boots's hands moved from his back to his shoulders as Brain shuffled backwards a few inches. "It's good now, thanks."

"You sure?" Boots didn't release his hold. "I'm here if you need me, Brian."

The use of his given name was surprising, an unexpected intimacy appearing to support the just-out-of-reach memories from last night. *Fuckin' head, first makin' it so I can't remember shit, and now it's pushing my wishes into play?* "I'm good, brother." He said it to remind himself of their relationship, which did not and would never include anything personal. He was a chore Boots had taken on, and that was all it could be. *Basically, I'm his job now.* "Hungry as hell, but I'm not dizzy no more."

Then Boots smiled, and that damn crooked tooth peeked out, and all Brain could think of was his mouth on Boots's. Shaking his hands out, he stepped back again, putting more space between them. A memory tugged at his attention, and he tried to ignore it, impossible as that seemed because the memory couldn't be anything except a dream from the adrenaline and meds. More evidence of his malfunctioning head. No way would Boots have pictures of men on his phone, yet Brain remembered holding the device, still warm from Boots's grip, and flicking through mouthwatering images. *They weren't nearly as impressive as Boots is,* he thought, and gasped.

"Head hurting all of a sudden?" Boots's hand landed on the back of his neck.

The hold felt so good, possessive, and supportive, Brain had to tuck his chin to his throat to hide from the man.

"No," he choked out, voice nearly unrecognizable. "I just—gimme a minute, yeah? I'll be down."

"Brain, are you hurting?" Boots was touching Brain's cheek with his other hand now, fingers stroking a slow path beside his ear. "I can stay—"

"No, I'm good." He wrenched free and turned his back on the man, chest heaving as he tried to catch his breath. He grabbed jeans from the floor, uncaring they were yesterday's wardrobe, and stuffed his feet and legs into them, pulling the clothing roughly up over his hips. "I'll be down, okay?"

Silence dragged on so long he thought Boots would reject the request, until he heard the scuff of a bare sole against the floor and knew the man was moving towards the door. "Okay, Brain." Boots's voice was soft and gentle, the hurt in it plain to hear. Brain fought against his sudden desire to ask the man to stay. "I'll start some food. You said you're hungry, right?"

"Yeah." He angled his head to look behind him, catching a worried glance from Boots. More quietly, he said, "I'm okay, Boots. I just need a minute."

Mouth pursed thoughtfully, Boots nodded and backed through the door, leaving it open as he walked out of sight down the hallway.

What the everlovin' fuck is wrong with me?

He couldn't out himself like this. Not that he'd heard any of the men say anything negative. Kirby had even invited the town's grocery store manager to one of their parties, and no one had blinked an eye when the man had shown up with his boyfriend. But the club members were fellow warriors, ex-military from every branch of service, all of them indoctrinated against the deviance of homosexuals, an expectation of weakness going hand in hand with same-sex attraction. That had been the military stance for so long, the need for men filling ranks making it so they accepted gays as long as they didn't advertise themselves. DADT-driven fear had made his desires into a dirty little secret, and even after the policy had been repealed, Brain hadn't been able to break ranks and say anything. *I can't lose the club.* He knew Kirby and the MBMC had saved his life, literally; otherwise, he would have eaten his gun before now.

What if Boots is fighting the same thoughts? He rolled his eyes at the idea of the hardened Vietnam vet being gay.

The man's just takin' care of a brother. "My brain's having itself a heyday. No pain, but lots of stupid fake memories. I need to forget this happened at all before it pisses me right off. Shit, I want and can't have, surefire way to get riled up."

Shaking out a folded T-shirt, he tried to convince himself of what was the most likely truth. He pulled the shirt on and dug out a pair of socks, dragging them on as he stood on one leg, then the other. Stomping into his boots, he looked down at the pillow beside his. *This is stupid.* He lifted the pillow with a jerky motion and inhaled a final time deeply, marking how it was exactly the same as Boots had smelled when he'd held him closely, steadying Brain through the worst of the dizziness. "I'm crazy."

As he swung around and out of the room, the last thought in his head was the knowledge that if he was going to start fantasizing about his club brothers this way, he needed to get to Texarkana, and soon.

Chapter Six
Old Boots

Poking at the scrambled eggs with a spatula, he tried to think of what he could do to come back from the unmitigated disaster the past ten minutes had become. *I shouldn't have touched him like that.* It was one thing to support Brain when he was dizzy and another to hold him close like a lover. Scowling down at the slow-cooking eggs, Clark abruptly shoved the flat of the spatula underneath and jabbed some more, loosening them from the bottom of the pan.

Shouldn't have done a lot of stuff.

He'd have to talk to Kirby today, tell him he'd be moving back into his own house down the street. In the past few months, he'd spent far fewer nights there than in the clubhouse. *At Kirby's request,* he reminded himself, knowing how shallow and fake it sounded even in his own head. *I just need some distance.* He nodded and scraped the eggs onto two plates. After setting the pan aside, he opened the microwave door and placed an extra layer of paper towels under the bacon before turning it on for another handful of seconds.

The stairs squeaked, and Clark released a deep breath, trying to push out all his nerves and tension with the air. He kept his back to the opening leading to the living area in the clubhouse and stared at the circling plate in the microwave until it beeped, signaling the cycle was complete.

"Hey." Brain sounded tentative, and Clark scowled down at the plates as he arranged bacon next to the eggs on each. "Smells good."

"Just breakfast food. Figured it'd be quick and easy." Clark opened a drawer and pulled out two forks, laying one on the counter, keeping the other in his grip as he picked up a plate. "There you go. I'm eating on the porch." Still without looking at Brain, he maneuvered past the man, careful to not touch him. "Enjoy."

"Boots?" Brain's voice was soft. The profound helplessness in the tone pulled Clark to a halt, hand frozen on the doorknob. "We okay?"

"Yeah, brother." He turned the knob and opened the door as he lied to Brain for the first time. "We're good."

Seated on the side porch, Clark methodically ate the food on his plate as he stared out at the quiet neighborhood. His house was in view, just past the next block's corner. The building sat on a small lot, which was fine with him, because he'd never been one for gardening. *Not like Dall.*

The bacon turned to ash in his mouth. Sometimes he would go for months without thinking about Dall, and here the man had invaded his mind twice in one day.

Older than Clark by nearly two decades, Randall Mayhan had been his friend and confidant, the two of them thick as thieves through the years. After things had changed between them, Clark had known the reasoning behind keeping things quiet and casual. Understood and supported Dall's demand. Men had been killed in small towns for less, and the culture of free love had never invaded Texas. Randall Mayhan had founded the town as a married man, fathering nine children on his loving wife—and from the first touch Clark had never looked at another man as long as his Dall had been alive. They'd set themselves up as best friends, staunch supporters for the other, and there'd never been a whisper of impropriety around their relationship. Not even as Clark had cared for Dall in his final days, with his wife long dead and his daughters and sons moved away. The nurses coming in and out without warning had forced Clark to keep his emotions at bay. At the funeral, he'd barely managed to keep himself under control, struggling to hold his salute through the services as he stood vigil at the foot of the grave.

Ten years later, the first time he'd gone out looking for a hookup had nearly killed him, but he'd wanted to touch someone, wanted to hold and be held, if only for a moment, even by a stranger.

I'm still a Buckler. His loyalty might have shifted, changing over to Kirby, Oscar, and the other new members, but the dogged support of the club itself had never wavered. Clark carried the half-finished plate into the kitchen, then scraped and rinsed it before placing it in the dishwasher. Then he returned to his chair outside and straightened to lean backwards, settling his feet against the porch railing.

Hours passed with the faint sound of video games coming from inside the house, balanced by voices that convinced him other brothers had Brain for now. They were all probably playing those damned first-person shooters the man liked so much. *Well, liked is probably the wrong word.* Even when the man was completely immersed in the game, Clark had watched as Brain took it upon himself to try to save his whole party. That wasn't enjoyment as much as it was self-flagellation, and he made a mental note to talk to Dominic Reed about it. Again. The club's staff counselor would know how best to approach things. *Not my forte,* he thought, and adjusted his position, feet still on the rail.

It was just before sunset, and the air had grown heavy with heat and moisture. *We'll have storms again tonight.* He remembered Brain's easy laughter after the meds had taken hold, how the man had teased him, not showing signs of having had an episode earlier in the night. *Need to get him to take his pills again.* Clark angled his head to rest against the high back of the chair. He sighed. "Maybe take a nap before it gets too late."

"I could nap."

The quiet voice held a thread of tamped back hope Clark didn't understand. He closed his eyes and bit down on the inside of his bottom lip until he tasted copper.

"I mean, I slept real good last night. Actually slept. Was the best rest I've had in a long time, but naps are always good, right?" Brain's question was soft and tentative, and Clark hated that the man felt like he couldn't ask for what he needed. *When did you ever ask for what you wanted, old man?* Pushing the thought aside, he turned to look up at Brain, who continued, "Docs are always tellin' me I can't get too much sleep. Good sleep."

As Brain hovered near the back of the chair next to Clark's, his fingers curled around the rungs, knuckles standing out in a stark white.

"You wanna nap?" Clark shifted his gaze to Brain's face, seeing how the man's eyes darted back and forth, glancing across his face before turning to the yard, then back again. *He wants this.* The way Brain had stared at the hookup app on his phone last night resurfaced in his head, the heated expression, the way his teeth had captured his bottom lip in a slow, sexy bite. "Let's see if we can nap." Clark stood slowly and groaned as he stretched to help ease the ache in his back, then walked past Brain and opened the door. "Come on, Brain." Standing back, he let the other man precede him into the house. On impulse, he held out his hand, shocked when Brain lunged towards it, grasping hold as if it were a lifesaver. He walked them to his downstairs bedroom, thankfully meeting no one along the way, the other men either out of the house or gathered in the media room.

Once inside, he thumbed the lock and flicked off the overhead light, leaving just the low glow from the bathroom window to light the way.

"Come on." He tugged, and Brain moved towards him easily. Clark raised a knee to the mattress and eased to the far side, putting pressure on the connection between them until Brain settled on the edge of the bed. *Rest of it needs to be his decision.* He relaxed his grip and separated from Brain, surprised the man allowed it. But only a breath later, he had an armful of lean, hard male body as Brain buried his face against Clark's neck. "It's okay, Brian. I've got you."

Brain's breathing stayed elevated, and Clark worried he'd hyperventilate. Then the sound stuttered and broke, Brain's shoulders shaking.

"Don't ask, don't tell's a real bitch, you know?" Brain's watery laugh held zero humor. "Down-low boyfriends and hookups don't make for a charmed life. It's stupid. I know it's the dumbest thing ever, but I didn't think I'd find anyone like me. Someone just trying to go along to get along, because they didn't want to lose the club, either."

"Hey, if this is your way of trying to out me—"

"What? No. Jesus, Boots. Hell no." Brain scooted backwards a few inches, looking up at Clark from underneath a sea of long, dark lashes spiked with tears. "I'm just..." He scoffed, the sound self-deprecating as he gestured at Clark. "You're you, and I'm just this whole entire mess." The distance between them evaporated as Brain burrowed close again. "You've been so nice to me, and I've had this ridiculous crush on what I thought was this unattainable straight man."

"A crush." He tested the words, finding they sounded just as absurd in his voice as they had in Brain's. "On me?"

"Not that I'm expecting anything." Heat from Brain's breath wafted over the skin of Clark's neck, setting up a chain reaction in his blood. "But I slept so good last night, and I thought maybe it wouldn't be weird if I asked you to hold me again." His voice was thin, thready, filled with trepidation. *He expects me to reject him outright.* "Just for one night. I won't ask again, Boots. I just didn't want to be alone tonight."

"I got you." *Oh, sweetheart.* Clark settled against the mattress, rolling to his back. He urged Brain to move with him and wound up with the man sprawled out over the top of him, head resting tight to the base of his throat. "You can sleep here." Awkwardly fumbling his phone out of his pocket, he woke it and navigated to the weather app. Holding it up, he squinted at it over Brain's shoulder, frowning at the radar. "Looks like less than an hour before the storms get here. What about your meds?"

"I took 'em already, little while ago. I watched you." There was the tiniest hitch in Brain's voice. "Was watching you. You were outside just sittin' there, and I ran upstairs and took the pills, just in case."

"Just in case?" He soothed down Brain's back with a palm, digging his fingertips in lightly on the upstroke as he set up a steady rhythm of comforting movement.

"Just in case you'd let me stay."

"Oh, my friend, I'll always try to do what's right by you." Clark tightened his hold on the man, doing his best to ignore the pure enjoyment of having Brain in his arms. "Just like last night."

"My head hasn't hurt all day." Brain burrowed a little closer, leg riding up high on Clark's thigh. "I'd forgot how good that felt. It's—it's been real bad the past few weeks, Boots."

"Well, let's see if we can get you another pain-free day." He curled the fingers of his other hand around Brain's neck. Clark grazed his thumb along Brain's jaw, smiling at the soft and smooth skin under his touch. "You shaved."

"Yeah." The answer was soft, barely a puff of air against his skin. "Wanted to look nice for you." The corners of Clark's mouth curved up again and he sighed quietly, still stroking up and down Brain's back. "You're real nice-lookin', could get anyone." Brain moved slightly, and Clark felt the brush of a hardened cock against his thigh. "Thought if I cleaned up, you might want me."

He's medicated. After seeing the pills' effects last night, Clark knew there was no way he would take advantage of Brain right now. Not and be able to live with himself tomorrow. They'd broken down every one of the man's walls and defenses, leaving him more real and bare than Brain probably even realized. *Hell, agreeing to this cuddlefest is probably stepping over the line.* But Clark would be damned before he would kick this man out of his bed. Not only were there storms coming, but holding Brain was no hardship.

"There's someone out there for you, Brian Nelson." Clark tipped his head and pressed a firm kiss to Brain's temple. The words stuck in his throat, but he pushed past an overwhelming reluctance to voice them, whispering encouragement that could as easily be applied to himself. "Just gotta be willing to put yourself out there a little bit and find him."

"Nah. It's scary out there."

"And in here? Not so scary anymore?" Brain laughed peacefully at Clark's question, scrubbing his cheek back and forth across Clark's chest as he shook his head. Clark tightened his hold on the man, telling him a piece of his truth. "Then I'm glad I can be your safe space tonight."

"Yeah, me too." Brain's gruff whisper barely stirred the air, but Clark caught the depth of meaning behind the few words, and he smiled.

They lay like that, still and quiet through the hours as the storm rolled in, lightning flashing through the sky as rolling thunder chased it from horizon to horizon. Brain's breathing never changed, stayed slow and even, Clark's hands finally settling into a gentle hold as the skies grew silent again.

He slept deeply and woke alone, back throbbing from holding one position all night.

Clark ignored how his empty arms ached, pushing that thought to the back of his mind as he started his day.

Chapter Seven
Brain

Staring at his hands, Brain mapped out the shakiness, noting how it was more prominent in his right than his left. *New development I should remember to tell the docs.* Even that little bit of weakness would suck for a ride, but he had to get out and away for at least a little while.

Brain had spent the past two days trying to blank his mind with video games. With the headset on and volume turned loud, he tried to ignore how it had felt waking wrapped around his crush. Guilt ate at him for how he'd left things, and since the tech gear also gave him a valid excuse to ignore anyone and everyone in the actual room with him, it all worked for Brain.

Not that Boots had forced anything. As far as Brain could tell, the man had zipped his lip about the weakness that had pushed Brain to Boots's bed. Gone dark and silent, hardly sticking his head into the clubhouse. And why shouldn't he? If Brain's shitty behavior got out to their brothers, the old man had just as much to lose as he did.

He'd woken this morning with a low-level headache. The symptoms had ramped up steadily throughout the day, the first ones he'd suffered since getting a couple nights of restorative sleep—and taking his meds. *Since I stayed with Boots.* He'd known the pain was coming on last night and had held the bottle of pills in his hand for a long time, staring down at the rattling tube of mind-numbing chemicals—then had gone to bed without taking any.

Grunting his lie to Kirby when asked later, Brain knew his white-knuckled reaction to the storms should have been a blatant tell. *No Boots to soothe everything over last night.*

The sudden absence had stung, more than expected, but Brain couldn't blame him for keeping his distance. *Forced my way into his bed, after all.*

But he couldn't take the meds and play his games, because the drugs fucked with his reactions and accuracy. That abstinence meant he'd been curled into a ball by midmorning. Pain shot from the back of his neck up and around his skull, piercing his eyeballs with sharp shards of agony.

After a second struggle with the idea of medicating, he'd tossed the bottle to the back of the nightstand drawer without taking any. *Out of sight, out of mind.* And that was going to be the motto of the day, because with a jovial Boots moving around inside the house joking as he made a late lunch for their brothers, Brain found himself needing to vacate the location.

Ignoring the tremors, he thumbed the start button on the bike and closed his eyes in reaction when the engine kicked over underneath him. The hellish noise and vibrations played additional havoc with his head, but getting in the wind was good for his mind, and he'd take that check on the plus side of the list every time.

Rolling away from the curb, he directed his front wheel towards the edge of town. He whipped the bike through the first set of curves on the highway. A broad grin played across his lips. *Needed this, big time.*

He'd left the clubhouse without a destination in mind but several rambling hours later found himself riding through the outskirts of Texarkana and decided to take the opportunity as fate.

The gay bar he most often frequented wasn't on a main drag through town. It was on the Arkansas-side outskirts, just outside the official city limits. When he heeled down his kickstand, he idly noted a mostly-hidden bike parked up near the side of the building but paid more attention to the high number of trucks and cars scattered around the lot. With enough men to choose from, he was nearly guaranteed a session with someone and found himself excited to get inside and see the options. As noisy as his brain had been, the promise of silence brought by a good orgasm made him eager.

He pocketed his key, fingertips finding the tiny silicone bag that held his traveling dose of meds. The pills were something Dominic had made him promise to never leave the clubhouse without—and he carried them faithfully. A futile gesture, because Brain would never take them outside a place he felt safe. *Which these days is just the clubhouse.* Fingertips digging into the skin of his forehead with a hard rub, he walked through the propped-open door and into noisy chaos. *Shit.* He hadn't been ready for the strobing lights but knew from experience if he kept his back to the dance floor, they wouldn't bother him too badly. He just had to make it the dozen strides or so to the bar that stretched along the backside of the club.

There was an empty stool about midway down the bar, and Brain eased his ass onto the poorly padded excuse for a seat. Give him a couple of beers, and he'd forget about his ass hurting—*unless it has a better reason to sting later*. Brain grinned and lifted a finger to the bartender, nodding towards the draft spigots.

Two minutes later, a perfectly drawn beer slipped onto a coaster in front of him, and Brain exchanged smiles with the bartender as he nudged a bill towards the man. "Keep 'em comin'," he called over the music, and the man nodded, turning to make change before returning to tuck the bills under the edge of the coaster. Taking a deep drink of the amber liquid, Brain smacked his lips in appreciation and angled his head to look down the bar to his left. Four couples and one single guy who must have already had too much to drink if the nearby mug of coffee was to be believed. *Well shit.* He'd hoped to find a likely candidate without having to approach the dance floor, but so far, that was a big nope.

Twisting the other direction, he saw ten men, all of whom were engaged in conversation with a neighbor. Body language told him most of them were either actively coupled or strongly attracted to their partner, but there were two guys down at the end who might be in the first-approach stage. The man facing Brain was younger, about his age. Decent-looking guy who was in shape but slender, with a tight tank top showing off toned arms. Twinks weren't really his type these days but might be good for a distraction.

The man with his back to Brain was a different story altogether. Maturity showing in the more salt-than-dark blond hair peeking out from underneath a ballcap, his broad shoulders strained the seams of the work shirt he wore. His sleeves were folded up midway over impressive forearms, and Brain allowed his gaze to linger on the inked skin peeking through, letting his mind wander to what the man might have hidden underneath his shirt. *Papa bear.* He hummed softly as he took a final deep drink of his beer before sliding the empty glass away to indicate he was ready for a refill.

The twink leaned closer and rested his palm on one of those bare forearms, and Brain sighed and resigned himself to continuing his search. Seemed the conversation was going the way at least one of the men desired, so he turned to face the bartender just as another full glass appeared. Nodding his thanks, Brain found an angle he could view the dance floor via a mirror without getting the strobes full-on and began to watch the tangled and grinding men, hands on hips, chest to back, touching their partners without fear. *Fuck, I wish I could do that.* Life would be easier if he could just get over himself, but old habits died hard.

The music changed to more of a slow dance, and he noted when two nearby stools were vacated, smiling down at his half-full beer as one man's eagerness left the stool spinning. It stopped when a large hand landed on the back, and from his peripheral vision, Brain saw a very fine ass settling onto the seat. He looked up with a joke on the tip of his tongue but nearly swallowed it when he recognized who was next to him.

Boots gave him a closed-lip smile as he folded his forearms along the rail of the bar. Bare, tattooed forearms that Brain had just been ogling. *Shit.*

"Can I buy you a beer?"

Out of all the starting gambits for this conversation, that was the last Brain would have expected. "Uh, I. Wha—"

"Relax, Brain. It's just a beer."

"Uh huh." *Just a beer in a gay bar.* "Sure."

That earned him a wider smile, and Brain's attention dialed down to focus on the flash of teeth before Boots turned to face the bartender. Beers apparently ordered—Brain would be damned if he could remember the bartender saying a word—Boots angled a glance in his direction again. That look seemed less confident, but this was Boots, here, and Brain's mind was entirely occupied with that idea.

"Before you ask, no, I didn't follow you here."

"I didn't think you had." Brain sipped his drink, resting his hands loosely around the chilled glass to hide the persistent trembling.

"I don't come here as often anymore, but the bar's been here for nearly as long as I remember, so I guess you could call me a longtime regular. Wasn't so blatant about preferred clientele in the beginning." Boots's arm flexed as he lifted his beer. Brain fixated on how the man's Adam's apple dipped with each swallow, muscles moving in his throat in a way that had Brain wanting to feel it with his mouth, his tongue, wanting to use his teeth along the column to mark him up just a little. "Testimony to how things change through the years. Never seen you in here, though."

"I—" He could lie and say it was his first time here, which was plausible. Everyone had a first time in any bar they entered. A newbie might not have known the makeup of the customers, an argument Brain could make easily. But this was Boots, and he deserved the truth. *He already knows. What's it matter at this point?* "I make it over here about once a month. More in the summer."

57

"Now, that wasn't so hard, was it?" Boots turned towards him, and the heated press of his leg against the side of Brain's was enough to have his dick chubbing up, uncoiling as it filled with blood.

A joke bounced around in his head, something he would have said to any other man in the bar if they'd given him a line like that, and he swallowed hard, thinking, *Fuck it.* "Not hard yet."

"Oh, that's bad. Ba dum tiss." He made the hand motions to match the drum sounds. "But I walked right into that one, didn't I?" Brain's breath caught in his throat as that damned crooked tooth was put on display for an instant. "Wonder how we've missed each other here. Must have been on different schedules, because I'm here at least once a month, too."

"You're—" He hesitated, because if he asked the question and Boots answered him, wouldn't he be required to give back the same information? *I told him the other night. Why should it be a big deal to say it now?* Brain picked up his beer and sipped, then kept his gaze on the glass as he centered it in the coaster, staying silent. *I just can't.*

"Gay? Yeah. It's okay, Brain. You don't have to say a thing. I saw you sitting here alone and wanted you to know you're not." Boots's leg brushed against him again, and the man's broad palm landed heavily on Brain's shoulder. "Alone, that is. I get it. Probably more than you can realize. I get why you don't want the boys to know."

"Does anyone know about you?" Brain shook his head, still trying to wrap his mind around the fact that Boots was here. Was here and gay and not freaking out about Brain being in the bar with him. *I'm not with him.* That thought pulled at something in his chest, and he tried to ignore the ache forming behind his breastbone. "Besides me, that is?"

"Kirby and Oscar. Kirb figured it out a long time ago, and Oscar needed to know why I couldn't give blood at that drive we did last year." Boots's fingers dug in, and Brain looked over at him, surprised at the frown on his face. "You seriously think our brothers give a fast shit about who we sleep with?"

"Well, yeah." Brain hated how confused he felt, but the fear and pain were doing a number on his head. "It's always mattered to men like us." Shaking his head, he corrected, "Like them."

"Oh, Brian." When Boots crooned his name, Brain turned to face him, liking how the man's thick thighs became wedged alongside his own, muscles flexing as Boots held him in place. "Lamb among wolves. 'Men like us?' I'm not sure what that even means anymore." The restricted movement had Brain's dick throbbing, and he shifted uncomfortably, trying to avoid reaching down to adjust himself. Just that was enough to catch even more of Boots's attention. The man's bottom lip rolled up and into his mouth, top teeth denting the soft flesh as he stared at Brain's erection. "Man like me, who likes what he sees, and thinks being open to an approach right now is all that matters."

"An approach?" Now Brain felt slow, unable to keep up with the topic changes. All available blood had centered in his dick, and if Boots piped up with an offer to hit the bathroom and rub one out, Brain would leave smoke behind moving fast enough the man wouldn't have time to change his mind.

"Yeah. Not a hookup, because you deserve more than that." Seemed Boots had other ideas. *Dammit.* "Something more certain and dependable. You're looking for a thing you can't even recognize, Brian, even if it's right in front of you."

"The guys wouldn't deal well with a relationship. Not something open." He shook his head, driving the idea far from the front of his brain, which was now clamoring for a chance. A possibility of something with Boots flashed in vignettes of them together at meals, at club events, in bed. *In bed. God, if only.* Lids sinking closed, he shook his head again, hard enough to rattle his pain-tortured brain. "I need the club. Can't do anything to jeopardize that, man. You don't understand."

"No, sweetheart, you're the one who doesn't understand. No one's going to give you grief if you come out. They won't care about who you love, just that you do. Just that you've got someone to hold when shit gets hard, because every one of us lives inside the same fucking nightmare at some point, and having someone to hold you when things suck is the only thing that keeps us going sometimes."

His mind stuck back on the unexpected "sweetheart," he blurted out, "Who do you have?"

As if his words embodied a physical presence plummeting between them, Boots leaned backwards, and his hand dropped from Brain's shoulder, emotion morphing his earnest expression and twisting it into something uncomfortable to witness. Boots's mouth opened and closed, his chin dropping heavily towards his chest, and then Brain was the one leaning in, a trembling hand resting on Boots's thigh, the other gripping his bare, muscular wrist, pulling them closer together.

"I don't have anyone." The muscles under Brain's hand flexed, turning to granite. "Not anymore." Boots's tone was completely different, generic and metered as the older man shook himself and stood, twisting away to pull out of Brain's grip while he yanked out his wallet. "Just wanted you to know that you're not alone, Brain. Okay? As long as you got that message, I'm good." Voice filled with gravel, low and pained, Boots tucked a couple of bills under his half-full glass and walked away. "See you later, brother."

Brain watched him go, frozen in place by the agony Boots had exposed, watching the man's back as he faded into the darkness outside. Pipes rattled, and a light speared through the parking lot, and before he realized what he was doing, Brain was on his feet and moving. He made it to the door just in time to see Boots's taillight heading up the highway. *Home. He's going home.*

Standing beside his bike, Brain clawed the key from his pocket, cursing when it flipped to the ground, immediately hidden by shadows. By the time he'd found it and started his own engine, Boots had disappeared. *I know where he's going, though. I can talk to him there.* They could finish this conversation at the clubhouse. Both of them had rooms, so privacy was guaranteed. He just had to force Boots to talk to him.

Now to convince himself he could have that conversation.

Chapter Eight
Old Boots

With his bike engine ticking behind him as it cooled off, Clark eased through the kitchen door and looked around, pausing to take in a breath of stale air. *Nothing's changed.* Going straight through to the main bedroom, he dropped everything from his pockets into an empty wooden bowl on top of the dresser. *Old habits die hard.* He made his way through the entire house, strategically opening windows, the decades spent living here more than enough to teach him which would catch a cooling wind but no water if storms happened to blow up unexpectedly.

The weatherman had claimed clear again for tonight at least, but this was East Texas, where the saying "if you don't like the weather, just wait" had been invented.

A ping and matching vibration from his phone had it back in his hand, gaze on the screen to see Kirby's **Enjoy your night** in response to Clark's earlier text that he was going back home for another few days. He hadn't had to say someone else would need to be responsible for Brain again, knowing it was implied.

Brain.

He pulled in a hard breath and blew back out the pain.

Brian.

Somehow they'd become different people in Clark's mind. Brain was the pain-in-the-ass brother who refused to help himself and Brian his gentler counterpart, the one who accepted support with good grace.

When Brian turned up at the bar tonight, Clark had no fear, no overriding anxiety that his ill-kept secret would be outed. No, he'd been stupidly excited, as if them being there at the same time was a sign. *More fool am I.* His first words had spooked the man, and throughout the brief conversation that followed, Brian's anxiety had grown. The unsettled reaction grew until there was nothing left of the cocky, loud, and laughing version of the veteran that had captured Clark's attention from the first time they'd met.

It had been nearly two years ago since he'd rolled out early on the morning all new members were supposed to ride to the club. Instead of a direct path, Clark had opted to route himself past the cemetery where so many of the original members now resided. By the time he'd made it back to the clubhouse, there'd been a party in full swing. Even though Oscar had kept him in the loop, it had been weird to walk in and see things so different from how Dall had kept them for years. Half of the men couldn't drink because of medications, and a certain other segment wouldn't, but he'd found a sinkful of ice and beer in the kitchen for the rest of them. Popping a top, he'd wandered through the crowd, introducing himself as he went.

There'd been a TV blaring in what Kirby had labeled the media room, so Clark had headed that direction and found a lone man seated on what looked like a comfortable couch, with a game controller in his hand. Grunts and head nods didn't count as conversation, so when the man wouldn't engage, Clark had positioned himself to be partially in the way of the screen. The man had remained focused so intently on the game he was playing, Clark had felt safe in looking his fill. The shifting colors and lighting changed his face's topography constantly, so Clark had been able to pick out bits and pieces like a strong jaw, square and with a layer of scruff, even as it was thrust forward antagonistically. A nose that had been broken more than once but still managed to look regal. A high forehead covered at times by an untamable mane of dark auburn hair. Good-looking hadn't covered the beauty of the man, and Clark had found he wanted to know more.

He remembered thinking, *Nothing good will come of obsessing over someone I can't have.* A futile sensation had swept over Clark, as it had so often since Dall's death, but as he'd turned to leave, the man had spoken for the first time.

65

"Where you goin'? Thought you were gonna keep me company." The game paused, and Clark glanced over his shoulder to see that face turned his direction for the first time. An unexpected vulnerability flashed over the man's expression, replaced in an instant by a flicker of pain. "I'm Nelson, Brian Nelson. You're one of the OGs, right?"

"Yeah, I'm an OG, no doubt." He turned back and thrust out his hand, ignoring the sting of being called old. "Clark Donaldson." Their palms met, and Clark felt a zap of energy he tried to laugh off. "You've got an electric personality."

"What do you think about the changes in the club? Think it's worth it to try and help an asshole like me?"

Nelson's response took him aback. Clark studied him for a moment, then asked, "You're an asshole?" He sat on the edge of the couch gingerly, then eased onto the cushions, careful of his back. "I hadn't noticed. I guess that comes out on the second meeting, no doubt. All you FNGs are the same, ready to ride in and tear shit up. Club wasn't broke and didn't need fixing, but I get what Kirby and Oscar are trying to do. Seems a worthy purpose."

"Hey, I'm no cherry. I've been around the block a time or two. The wrong block, as it turned out, but whatever." Brian lifted a shoulder as he leaned back, sitting closer to Clark than he'd been a moment before. "Wanna play with me?"

Clark buried the smile and quip that begged to be released, opting to instead shake his head in a quick refusal. "Games aren't really my thing."

"Your loss." Brian focused on the screen again. "Oh, man. They've got all the new shit. This is an FPS I've been looking forward to playing."

"FPS?" When Brian laughed aloud, he wished he'd kept his mouth shut instead of asking.

"OG, man. Serious OG. FPS is first-person shooter. It's the kind of game I like the best." The screen changed, and scenery rushed at them, the unseen character Brian controlled racing through the environment, leaping and climbing in instinctive movements. "It's like I'm inside the game sometimes. Gets me out of my head."

"You get stuck in your head a lot?"

"Yeah, my brain got scrambled. I've got some shit goin' on, old man. You would not understand."

Clark suppressed another grin. "You'd be surprised. You know the old guard are all vets, right?"

"Even you, with your pretty face?" Clark forced himself not to react to that statement, continuing to stare at the TV. "You can't be that old. Hard to see you in a helmet and fatigues."

"I did my time in the jungle. No dry heat for us. And instead of IEDs, we had tunnels and tripwires to deal with. Turned sixty-four couple of months ago." The game's

67

character rounded a corner, encountered an overwhelming enemy force, and was wiped out in seconds. The in-game perspective changed as the figure fell to its back, sky spinning to darkness overhead. "Did you just die in the game?"

"Yeah." Brian shrugged. "Shit happens. At least in the game I can respawn. I'm forty." Sure enough, the screen changed back to the beginning of the sequence, and the scenery started rushing at them again as Brian moved through the obstacles faster. "You sure you don't want to play? You're not that old."

"Nah, not my speed. But I can keep you company." He settled into the cushions, lifting his now-warm beer to finish the can. "No problem."

But it had become a problem. Brian had quickly earned the moniker Brain, which he'd claimed to like better than the Nelson sewn to his vest, and he'd renamed Clark Old Boots, claiming he needed a way to remember to be respectful to his elders. After a few months, the games had become everything, something Brain would play without sleeping or eating. According to the club's counselor, an addiction to the sense of power and movement wasn't surprising. Brian's head needed patterns, and game progression provided that in spades, with little cause-and-effect consequences. His characters became crusaders in the game, leading teams to save other combatants and innocents. *Also not surprising.*

Then had come the flashbacks, seemingly appearing out of nowhere one night during a storm. Brian had trashed his room fighting ghosts, and Kirby had asked various club members to become the man's minder, watching over him. Not in so many words, but the frustration Kirby and Oscar felt at the broken furniture and holes in the wall was balanced by a sincere desire to help the man they'd all come to know so well.

The better Clark had gotten to know Brian, the more he'd liked him, finding the man's challenges weren't an issue. Clark had gradually found a rhythm to the nightmares, and as he took responsibility for Brain, he'd settled on a solution and then worked to find a way to implement it. With the counselor's support, he'd forced Brian to cut back on the games, pulling the man into other activities in the clubhouse, helping him build relationships with the rest of the members.

And it was going so well.

He scoffed far back in his throat and opened the refrigerator, not surprised to find it nearly empty. *At least there are no science experiments to toss.* Opening a drawer next to the stove, he pulled out a handful of takeout menus, quickly sorting them into pickup and delivery. A glance through the options had him retreating to the bedroom to reclaim his phone. He ignored the many messages on the screen as he opened the device, heading directly to the actual phone option. Pizza ordered, he shoved the menus back into their drawer and opened the freezer. The half-full bottle of vodka lying on its side earned a grunt of approval, and Clark retrieved it, closing the door as he opened a cabinet with his other hand, not wanting to wait a moment longer than necessary to feel the bite of the liquor. He splashed an inch of liquid into the old jelly glass, then lifted it and tossed it back, blowing out a breath of satisfaction as it burned all the way down to his belly. Another larger flow of liquid made its way into the glass before he recapped the bottle, putting it back into the freezer.

Walking through his house, he found himself oddly unsettled, not able to focus on anything, just moving from window to window, lifting the glass for an occasional sip. Lights swept across the front of the house, and he detoured through the bedroom again, swapping the glass for his wallet before going to the side door.

"Hey, Mr. Donaldson." The mayor's son opened the insulated pizza carrier and retrieved the square cardboard box.

"Keep the change." He shoved a bill at the boy and took the box in return. "Have a good night."

"Oh, hey, thanks, Mr. Donaldson. You have a good night, too," the boy called over his shoulder as he sprinted towards the car, probably afraid Clark would change his mind about the size of the tip.

He grinned as he shoved the door closed, automatically twisting the bolt lock into place. After dropping the pizza off in the kitchen, he went to the bedroom. Once again, he exchanged his wallet for the glass, going straight to the freezer to replenish the level of liquor. *Need to not get drunk. What if Brian—* His first instinct was to immediately put the brakes on, but he cut the thought off in midstream.

I can get drunk as I want. Nobody's depending on me tonight.

Chapter Nine

Brain

"What do you mean? Boots ain't here? Where the hell is he?" Brain's face twisted until he was glaring at Oscar, the focus spiking an ache behind his eyes. He knew he was getting loud, but didn't care. The whole ride from Texarkana to home—and wasn't it fucked up to call a communal house "home"—he'd planned out what he'd say to Boots, explain his side of things. *All I need is twenty minutes with him.* "Man isn't here, shouldn't we be on the horn lookin' for him?"

Oscar's steady regard ought to have humbled him, but Brain's anxiety spiked, and a bolt of pain blew through the top of his head, causing him to lean sideways and grip the countertop to keep from staggering. It felt like he'd been asking the same question for hours, from the moment he'd gotten home to find Boots not present and surely not accounted for.

Oscar's shoulders lifted as he spoke. "He's taking a few more days. That's all I know. I didn't talk to him, Brain. What I got, I got from Kirby, so I'm assuming Boots contacted him directly."

"A few days? More days?" Iron bands tightened around his chest until he couldn't pull in a full breath. "Days? As in plural?" Since he'd first come to Mayhan and the club, Brain didn't think he'd ever gone more than twenty-four hours without Boots being around. He was the definition of a steady Eddie. "What if..." Brain swallowed, the spit somehow turning into a lead ball in his throat, growing larger with every aborted gulp, trying to choke him. "Are there storms tonight?"

Fumbling his phone from his front pocket, he first had it upside down, then turned the wrong direction. Each change in position required more dexterity than his fingers seemed to own, and Brain turned his back on Oscar to hide the way his hands shook. Resting the device on the countertop, he clasped his wrist with his other hand in an attempt to control the sudden onset of tremors worse than anything he'd ever dealt with.

The weather app finally opened, and he tried to breathe out a sigh of relief at the clear forecast, but the weight and pressure on his chest had it come out a keening whine.

Heat and weight in the shape of a hand rested on his shoulder, and he struggled to twitch away, not wanting the pity attention Oscar was trying to give him. It was a futile attempt, because Oscar wouldn't let him go.

"Few days, huh?" As he flicked to the next day, the little breath he had drawn in oozed out of him at the lightning and clouds depicted. The high double-digit percentage underneath hammered the last nail home in his coffin. *Oscar knows about Boots. He told me so. He's not going to care.* "I don't know if I can do this without him."

"I can stay with you. Lindy and Chris can come over for dinner. She likes seeing everyone." Oscar dug into the muscles of Brain's shoulder as he talked about his wife and son. "Not a hardship to play a few games, Brain."

Brain bent double at the waist, hands flat on the counter as he pushed his body backwards, finally getting out from under the unwelcome physical touch. Staring at the floor, he repeated, "I don't know if I can do this without him, brother. It's not just the games, man. I need him. Call him and tell him I need him back here." He tried to slow his panting, only marginally successful as he rolled his fingers into fists and pounded on the countertop. "Get him back here. *Now*."

"I know he sits with you at night sometimes. Saw the chair in your room. Won't kill me to park my ass there tonight if you need me, Brain." Oscar moved, and Brain lifted his head to find him across the island, noting the man had wisely moved out of reach. "But he went home for a reason. Man spends most of his life here now, and when he asks for a reprieve and to go to his own home for a change, we don't naysay him. The club is a calling for me and Kirby, and we don't expect him to be the same. Hell, he quit his job to help us out, and we don't pay him a damn thing. If he needs to step back for whatever reason, we respect that desire and him, and he gets to step back. That means you put up with me, and if you can't stand me—no offense taken, I promise—then we get one of the other brothers to help out as needed." Oscar shook his head. "What we don't do is call Clark—Boots—and tell him to get his ass back over here. He's earned the right to do whatever makes him happy."

Brain unfolded and stared at Oscar, reprocessing the words back through to make sense of them. *Home? He has a house here in town?* No, Oscar hadn't said Boots's house was in Mayhan, but it made the most sense. *Quit his job?* Had he quit to be available to Brain? He was the one who demanded most of Boots's time, the other brothers only occasionally asking him to drive them to appointments and stuff. Mostly Boots was here because Brain was. *And now he's not. Because of me.* "Call him. Please, call him and ask if I can just see him a minute. I'll meet him wherever. Just..." Brain closed his eyes, lids dropping slowly. "My head's pounding, man. He makes me better. I did something earlier today, and I hurt him. Swear, I didn't mean to." He hated the way his voice echoed through the room, hated he was yelling at Oscar. "Tell him I didn't mean to. I just need to see him, dammit."

"Keep it down a little, brother." Kirby spoke from the opening to the living area of the house. "Shoutin' the house down, Brain." The tone was light, but Kirby's voice was tight with an anxiety Brain recognized. The way everyone but Boots was around him when he was having his headaches. Like he could explode at any moment. "Let me get your meds."

"No, I don't want the meds." Brain hated how he sounded, the petulant whine in his voice. "I want Boots."

"He's not here, brother."

"Jesus, I fuckin' know he's not here. Because of me. Because of how I am." Brain bent double again, head thudding hard against the countertop's edge. That didn't add much to the hurting, so he did it a second time, then a third. "Because of me. Because of me."

"Get the meds." Oscar's voice came from right beside Brain, and something cushioned the next hard thump of his head against the countertop. "I've got him." Arms circled Brain and pulled him upright, but he refused to open his eyes. "Come on, Brain."

He balked at the stairs, refusing to lift a foot to go up, knowing if he were locked in his tiny room, he'd go insane. Hands turned his body, and he stumbled at the shift in direction. Then Oscar was urging him faster, Brain's feet tangling at the quick pace. They turned again, and something hit the back of his calves, forcing his knees to bend, and he sat back on a cushioned surface.

"I'll apologize to him later for using his room." Oscar's words didn't make sense through the noise in Brain's head, the pain rushing in with crashing agony that thundered through his skull.

Hands opened his mouth, and the tablets placed on the back of his tongue triggered an automatic swallowing reflex; those had become such commonplace actions they were no longer worth even noting. He leaned sideways and dropped his head against thick padding, rolling away from the light to bury his face into the softness. Only then did he recognize the smell and grab the pillow close to inhale deeply. A second hard pull of the scent into his lungs had the bands around his chest easing somewhat, and a third dislodged the boulder in his throat. He kept doing that, just breathing in Boots with every deep draught of air, until the medication took hold, slipping him beneath the level of true awareness and leaving him with only dreams.

Dreams in which he shared a house with Boots, and everyone knew who he loved.

Chapter Ten
Old Boots

Pain woke him, the perfectly timed thudding of his temples marching alongside the nausea swelling in his middle. "Damn." Eyes tightly closed, he stretched with a groan before he swung his legs off the bed and sat on the edge, fighting the sparks of pain in his back. Straightening the T-shirt he'd slept in, he muttered, "I'm too old for this shit." *Too old for a lot of things.* Fumbling around on the nightstand allowed him to find his phone by touch, and he brought it close to his face as he forced one bleary eye open just a sliver.

It took a few blinks to focus, but midmorning wasn't too late, even if it was hours after he'd normally have been up and at whatever his goals were for the day.

Today he didn't have any ambition, so sleeping in wasn't a crime. Being at loose ends wasn't something he enjoyed as a rule, but one day wouldn't kill him.

He unlocked the device as he yawned, then thumbed through a couple of screens to the message icon where he had several notifications. Steeling himself, he tapped the app, surprised to see messages from Kirby, Oscar, and Brain. There hadn't been any storms last night, and he would have expected they'd have a quiet night of it, so he frowned when Oscar's messages were a list of what he'd done to help Brain through an episode. In response to the message apologizing for using his room because it was a better solution, whatever that meant, Clark tapped out a quick: **No problem**.

Moving to Kirby's messages, he read the first, then paused, reading it a second time because it just didn't make any sense: **Know you like your privacy, old man, but you dropped a mess in my lap this time.**

The next didn't offer any clarity, muddying the waters even more: **Not like you to run from something. I thought you were better than that.**

"Boy, I half raised your ass. You need to watch that mouth before it trips you straight into trouble." Clark decided the rest of the messages could wait until he had at least one cup of coffee in him. He snagged a pair of sweatpants from where they were draped across the foot of the bed and put them on, pulling them up as he stood. The nausea had receded, for which he was grateful, but the pain in his back persisted enough that he trailed a hand along the wall as he walked to the kitchen.

He thanked his foresight in preparing the pot as he turned the switch on, standing and staring until the first trickle of dark liquid filled the bottom of the carafe. Knowing the only thing in the refrigerator was the box of leftover pizza, he opened the pantry door and surveyed the meager offerings. "Oatmeal it is." The instant packets tasted like salty cement, but it would put something in his belly to offset the acidity of the coffee he planned on drinking by the bucketful today.

Ten minutes later and he was seated on a padded chair on his back patio, bare feet propped on the rail as he alternated between the warm bowl of oatmeal and the hot mug of coffee. There was a concerning heaviness in the air, a dark line of clouds crawling along the western horizon that promised activity later in the day. He idly thumbed the button on the phone to unlock it, bowl cradled in his lap as he lifted the coffee in his other hand. The weather app had an exclamation mark next to it, which didn't bode well for today. Inside, the news was even worse. With storm watches already in play and only a couple of counties to the west, they were under warnings for tornados, flooding, and storms.

He pushed the phone button, then dialed a number from memory, not bothering to go to his favorites. It rang twice, and Kirby answered with a muted, "Hello?"

Clark ignored the odd hush, getting straight to the business driving him to make this call. "Did you see the weather forecast? Brain's going to need to take his meds now, and then the second dose midafternoon. I know he hates that shit, but it's going to be bad, Kirb."

"Yeah, I saw the alerts earlier. You just rollin' out of bed, old man?" There was noise in the background, and Kirby muttered, "Oh, shit," his voice getting fainter as if he had moved away from the phone.

"Where are you, Boots?" The shout took him by surprise. Brain was on the phone, and Clark let his lids drift closed, blocking out the view of his overgrown flowerbeds and yard to focus on Brain's voice. "Where the hell did you go yesterday? I got back here to talk to you, and y-y-you weren't here." The vulnerable tone wasn't something he'd heard from Brain before, and Clark's shoulders dropped in guilt. "You weren't here."

"I came home." He swallowed another sip of coffee and leaned sideways to place the mug on the floor. "I just needed—"

The oatmeal in his lap tipped, and he dropped the mug in a failed attempt to catch the bowl. Both smashed as they hit the floor—then a massive wave of pain locked his muscles, and he fell, sharp pain piercing his thigh as he landed on the broken crockery. Shaking his head, he stared at the wet and growing red patch on his leg. "Shit." The pain in his back hit again, and he tipped backwards, not able to get his elbows underneath him in time, skull bouncing off the hard concrete with an oath-inducing thud. Something buzzed nearby, and he waved at it, hoping the day wouldn't be made worse with a wasp sting.

"Damn." He blinked up at the rafters as he lay back on the floor, waiting for the world to stop waving along the edges of his vision. It took a while, but eventually, he felt stable enough to push up on an elbow. The red now stained the concrete in a small puddle around his hip, and he stared at the white splinter protruding from the side of his leg. "Huh." He scooted backwards until he could lean against the back wall of the house, then clamped one hand around where the shard had embedded itself, ignoring the pain as he yanked it out and tossed it to the side.

The buzzing noise was back, and his gaze landed on his phone vibrating sideways. *Must have hung up when I fell.* He felt bad for worrying them, but he had enough to deal with without Kirby or Oscar hovering and making things out to be a dozen times worse than they were. They'd been good kids who'd grown into great men, but they shared one trait with their grandfather—they were both worriers.

"Boots?" That shout came from the front yard and was followed by thudding that had to be fists trying to batter down his front door. *How the hell does Brain know where I live?* "Boots!"

"I'm back here, Brian." Clark didn't like how weak his voice sounded, so he tried again. "Around the back."

Seconds later, Brain rounded the corner and was on the patio, landing on his knees next to Clark. "What happened?" He looked and sounded alarmed and out of breath, chest heaving as color rode high on his cheeks. "You cried out, and then the call disconnected. Shit, man, you're bleeding."

"Yeah, I see that." Clark aimed at amused but suspected he'd missed the mark when Brain's expression morphed from terrified to angry, the emotional volatility telling Clark a lot about how the man's night had been. "Help me up and inside, would ya? Cut myself on a tiny piece of coffee mug. I'll clean this mess up later." He held out a hand and waited. Futilely, which was frustrating.

Gaze still on the redness saturating Clark's sweatpants, Brain asked, "Shouldn't we get a doc to look at you?"

"Boy," he drawled slowly, putting as much authority in his voice as possible, "I've had worse places on my eyeball. Just get me up and inside, and I can take care of my own self. Don't need no doctor for a tiny thing like this."

"Boots?" The shout was followed by another round of assaults against his front door, and Clark groaned as Oscar continued to yell.

Brain shook himself like a dog, and his jaw tensed, muscles in his cheek and neck flexing. "Around back," he called loudly, then picked up Clark's phone when it started vibrating again. "Kirby, he's hurt. I think he needs a doc."

"I do not need a doc," Clark said loudly. "What I need is someone to damn well help me off the floor so I can get cleaned up." Oscar appeared at the steps leading up to the patio, and Clark sighed. "Finally, someone with some sense. Oscar, son, help me get up. I pulled the damn thing out but want to get a look at the damage so I can deal with it."

"Don't touch him." Brain's statement was flat, filled with an anxiety and anger Clark hadn't heard from him before. "I don't think I can deal if you touch him."

"I won't touch him, Brain. Promise you that. Hand me the phone. Let me talk to Kirby," Oscar said, staring down at Clark. "Then you can help Boots."

"That's what I've been saying." Clark loosened the grip he had on his leg, surprised at the tiny spurt of blood that flooded out between his fingers. "Aw, shit." He looked up, ready to accept assistance, but Brain had different ideas.

Hands gripped his upper arms and lifted, sliding his back up the wall. He struggled to get his feet underneath him, the position awkward to keep the pressure on the wound, but Clark wasn't going to complain. At least he was off the floor. The world swayed, and he leaned forward, aching head and one shoulder pressed against Brain's chest while arms circled around him as another spasm wracked the muscles alongside his low spine.

"Back hurts. That's why I fell," he admitted, keeping his voice low.

"You're a damn stubborn man, Uncle Clark." Oscar's words meant Clark hadn't been as quiet as intended, and he winced at the man pulling out an old mode of address.

"Brain, now that you're holding on to him, can I touch him? Let me just rip the opening a little more so I can see the wound. That'll tell me what our next steps are."

"Yeah." The steady rise and fall of the chest under Clark's cheek didn't change, and he leaned in, giving Brain a little more of his weight. "It's good now. Go for it, brother."

Oscar crouched nearby, and Clark felt a tug at the fabric, followed by the distinct sound of threads separating. "Positioning isn't bad, no likelihood of any arteries being involved, but with this much blood, it definitely punched through something. You're going to need stitches, Uncle Clark. I can get our doc here, or we can go to the clinic." Oscar snorted. "Or the ER. Your call on where, but not your call on the what. This needs professional management, hear me?"

"You're a pain in my ass, boy." Brain's chest moved in shuddery jerks, and there were matching puffs of air against the top of his head. "Don't think you're immune to my ire, Brian. Don't be an ass."

"Yes, sir," Brain strangled out, then laughed softly. "Want to sit down out here and wait for the doc?"

"Yeah." He lifted his head, shocked at how close Brain's face was. His lips were right there, a strained smile pulling them crooked. Brain also had dark circles under his eyes, proof that even though there hadn't been storms, he'd still had a rough night. "You okay, Brian?"

"I wasn't, but I am now." The arms around him tightened, pulling him closer. "More right than I knew I could be."

Clark stared, watching as the smile on Brain's face turned into an honest one, sweet and filled with an emotion that frightened him. Lines of tension disappeared, and he could swear the boy looked a decade younger in that moment, handsome and effortlessly engaging. In an instant, Clark knew he'd do anything to get to know him better. Would follow him anywhere. Keep him. *If only he were mine.*

Clearing his throat, he pulled his gaze away with effort and looked down at the overturned chair. "Oscar, make yourself useful, straighten that up so I can sit, son."

Instead of just putting the chair back in place, Oscar brought it over, and Brain helped Clark shuffle forward a step so it could fit behind him.

"Okay, go easy so I can keep hold of my leg." Brain handled him delicately, as if Clark could break apart at any moment, and he tried to stuff down emotions the tenderness invoked, focusing on getting his ass into the seat without losing his balance again. "There we are, I'm good now."

The arms didn't release him, and instead of moving away, Brain crowded closer, his head going to Clark's shoulder. When the man made a choked-off gasp, Clark instinctively gripped the back of his neck, fully aware of how it would look to anyone entering the back yard.

"It's okay, Brian. I'm good now—" The word he wanted to say stuck in his throat, and he compensated by leaning his head against Brain's. Mouth to his ear, Clark breathed out slowly, then told him what felt right, "I'm okay, sweetheart. Swear. I'll be okay."

"You sure, Clark? I don't think I could manage if—" Brain's voice hitched, and Clark tightened his fingers again, setting up a rhythm to his grip and release, making it more of a massage than holding this man to him. "I need you." Lower, rougher, "I want you."

Closing his eyes, Clark responded with the truth, as he'd promised Brain he would always do.

"I want you too."

Chapter Eleven
Brain

Those words were going to be branded into his mind, playing on an endless loop of amazement. *"I want you too."* When he'd woken in Boots's bed for the second time back at the clubhouse, he'd lain there, pillows clutched to his chest as he tried to make sense of the previous evening. After arriving home and not being able to locate Boots, he'd gone a little crazy, his emotions on a roller coaster.

The entire way back from Texarkana, he'd put together and practiced a depressing-as-shit speech in his head, one where he explained to Boots that coming out wasn't going to happen. That maybe—*maybe*—they could have some private fun between the sheets, but that would be the extent of things. He'd waxed eloquently about how their brothers would never accept them together, words woven through with the certainty he held close.

Then he'd gotten home, and Boots hadn't been there. For half an hour he'd argued with himself that the concern he felt was the same as he'd have for anyone in his life who might be in trouble. Nothing more, nothing less. But as more time went by without the familiar and distinctive rumble of Boots's bike outside, it had become difficult to feed himself that same lie.

When he'd finally accepted the truth of his feelings, it had struck him hard, a brutal realization that his heart was hurting more than his head ever had. Worry about Boots and fear of what him not being there might mean had ratcheted up his anxiety levels until he could feel himself spiraling out of control, unable to stop things from getting to that point and beyond. Fortunately for him, Oscar and Kirby had been right there, helping him hold things together as best they could. It might have been chance that'd had Oscar bedding him down in Boots's room, but the way those two cousins worked, maybe not.

After waking curled on Boots's bed, Brain had showered in the man's bathroom, shamelessly filling his hand with bodywash from the shelf just to get another hit of familiarity. The action of wrapping that hand around his dick, thrusting through the slick that smelled of home and love wasn't something he could have stopped. Not until he'd striped the walls with evidence of his obsession. The realization that Kirby and Oscar knew Clark was gay had resurfaced, and he'd exited the shower quickly after that. Sprinting up the stairs dressed only in a towel, he'd been on a mission to get clean clothes from his own room so he could begin the search for Boots in earnest.

Back downstairs, he'd motioned Kirby into the clubhouse manager's office and stood in a close approximation to attention. That had lasted only until Kirby had rolled his eyes, calling a sardonic "at ease" that had still felt like permission, and then Lord how Brain's mouth had flowed. He knew his side of the conversation had been choppy, aggravated at how he'd kept getting ahead of the story, having to circle back around and fill in the gaps until Kirby had held up his hands. Brain had obeyed the order and immediately closed his mouth, waiting.

"Brother." The two softly spoken syllables were as comforting as a blanket wrapped around him, and he breathed out an easy sigh. "You're a Buckler. Hand selected, man. Did you really think so little of me to assume I'd kick you to the curb for anything short of betrayal? Much less who you want or like? My grandfather had a companion after my grandmother died, and one of the things I remember best was his staunch defense of that relationship. With a man, in case I need to spell it out. Family and club members knew, and Pops always said, 'Damn the rest of the world.' He wasn't one for labels, and I'm not either. You like who you like, brother, and that's just part of you. Sort of how your service, eye color, choice of video games, or that damned insistence on not eating green vegetables are all just aspects of what makes you the asshole we know and love." Kirby grimaced. "I'd say I'm offended, but I totally get where you're coming from. The government's good at doing that double-standards shit and making it seem like their way is normal and reasonable. But you and I both know in the real world, most of their shit

don't fly. Look at what they say is acceptable treatment for PTSD, which is nothing but shit. Men need a multi-faceted treatment, not just pills thrown at them and bored talking heads repeating the same old tired spiel. So, no." Kirby *leaned forwards, palms pressing flat on the desk between them. "You being gay won't be an automatic ticket to the door. Never. Brother, you're a Buckler, and that shit's for life, man."*

Then Kirby's phone had rung, and he'd taken one look at the screen and pointed at the door. Brain had been halfway out when he'd overheard the hushed conversation and realized who was on the other end of that call.

And that led him directly here, on one knee next to where Clark sat in a chair on the back patio of his personal house, the doc who worked part-time at the clubhouse currently stitching up the wound in Clark's leg.

Brain had no idea what came next, but he knew getting the address out of Kirby had been a turning point, because the man wouldn't have sent him here if he hadn't believed Brain belonged. At least in the club, caring for their brothers…but maybe more. Maybe he even thought Brain belonged exactly where he was, next to this man who made him feel so much. Safe, sure, which had been the beginning. But there were so many aspects to this beautiful feeling welling up inside him. Admiration, concern, affection, and yes, lust, because he couldn't think about Clark without his cock getting stiff.

"I'll be fine on my own." Clark waved a bloodstained hand through the air, not realizing the display was a surprisingly good argument *against* his stance of self-sufficiency. "Seriously, I just need some food and a pain pill. I drank more than is advised last night. No big deal."

"Why don't you let me be the judge of that." The doctor's voice was quiet and even, but his tone was granite, and Brain was glad to hear it. If he let the good doctor do the arguing, it meant he'd be lower on Clark's shit list at the end of things. "Then we'll see what kind of care's dictated. You hit your head pretty hard, based on the goose egg already raising."

"You hit your head?" Brian gave Clark's forearm a squeeze. "I didn't know that."

"It's not a big deal. My back seized up because I forgot to take my meds. I was just...out of sorts last night." Clark shifted in the chair, and the doctor's hands chased the wound, working on the moving target as if that were normal. "I was stiff and sore out of the gate this morning and needed food in my belly before I could take the pills. Which was why I was trying to eat breakfast when I got distracted and took my tumble." His red-coated fingers landed on top of Brian's hand and gave it a pat. "I'm fine, Brian. Nothing for you to worry about." Clark turned to look at him. "Weather's coming in tonight. Did you take your meds this morning?"

"We're not focused on me right now, Clark." He watched as the man's eyes widened at the use of his given name, something Brian hadn't used before today. "Let's get you squared away before we take on additional challenges." Looking over at the doctor, who was leaning back and studying Clark's thigh, he asked, "You done, Doc? He okay to walk inside?"

"Should be. I want to give you some instructions on what to watch for with his head, but then you can help him get cleaned up. Only a quick shower because we don't want to soak the sutures. Don't let him strain the muscles around the area, or he'll start bleeding again. He's already done more of that than he needs to for the day." The doctor stood, tugging off the nitrile gloves, then tucked them into each other until they made a tidy ball as he scooped up the bits of packaging near his feet.

"*He* is right here and can speak for himself, thank you very much." Clark bent and put his elbows on his knees. "I'm not powerless, and I've gone a long time now being the only one caring for myself." Head bowed, he looked at the floor between his still-bare feet. "Still. I wouldn't turn down some help back into the house."

"What do I do for the pain?" Brian ignored Clark's huff of annoyance and stared at the doctor, who was looking between the two of them with interest. "What does he need?"

"Again, *he* is right here, Brian." Clark moved so he was in Brian's line of sight. "I need to eat something, and then I'll take my pills and lie down for a while." He grimaced. "I

MariaLisa deMora

don't have much in the house for food, so I'll be rearranging that schedule to include hitting the store first."

"What can I get at the grocery store? What do you like?"

"I know what Uncle Clark typically buys," Oscar interjected. "Done enough grocery runs with him through the years. I can pick up everything and be back here in thirty minutes. He's probably got some candy in there. The man loves suckers, so he can start with that. It's better if you stay with him, Brian." Oscar stood from where he'd been sitting on the steps. "I'll do my part while you get Uncle Clark inside. Don't worry about the glass and stuff out here. I'll finish cleaning up when everything's sorted."

"Come on, Clark." Brian stood and held out a hand. "First you can show me where the secret sugar stash is, and then I hear a shower calling your name." Clark stared up at him, the expression on his face exposing a rare moment of uncertainty. This was a man far more accustomed to taking care of others. No matter what, it wasn't going to sit easy for him to be the one to need help. Feeling bold, Brian leaned close and murmured, "Do what you're told, and you might get a little bit lucky in the shower, old man."

"And I'm getting up right now." The grin on Clark's face was broad and real, the corners of his eyes crinkling as he took Brian's hand. "Doc, send me your bill."

"No charge for members, you know the drill. Thank you for your service." The doctor stepped out of the way as Brian pulled Clark to his feet. Oscar had already

94

disappeared around the corner of the house. "Clark, it looks like you're in capable hands, so I'm going to head out. Watch that pain and stay on top of it for a couple of days. Make sure you aren't heading into a new phase. And that head worries me, so if you have worse than normal headaches or any residual dizziness, you need to check in so we can deal with things before anything gets grim."

"Yeah, yeah. I know the drill." Clark waved as Brian slipped an arm around his waist to keep him steady. "I'll let you know." The taller man leaned against Brian, who readily accepted the burden, guiding him to the door as the doctor followed Oscar's path around the corner of the house and out of sight. "I'm really okay, Brian. You don't have to stay."

"I'm staying right here. Gonna have to deal with it, Clark." He turned sideways and edged through the door, pulling Clark's body tighter against his.

His first impression of the house was comfort, the muted colors harmonious together and an inviting overstuffed sofa and chair set visible through the archway. The kitchen itself had a massive island with four stools tucked along one edge. The appliances were somewhat dated, but not ancient, and matched the ambiance of the entire house. A home, someplace he could see as solace at the end of a long day. Somewhere to be comfortable with a partner.

"Get me to the sink first. I wanna wash up." Brian stayed pressed along Clark's side, watching as he turned on the water faucet, flicking fingers through the stream of water for a few seconds until it apparently achieved an acceptable temperature. Brian liked the closeness, probably too much, but couldn't make himself move away.

When Clark was casually drying his hands on a kitchen towel, Brian asked, "Where'd you hide your candy stash?"

"End drawer on the other side of the island." Brian hooked a stool out and supported Clark's weight as he settled down with a soft groan. "Grab a yellow one. They're my favorites."

Keeping one eye on Clark, he opened the drawer and grinned at the container inside. The plastic bowl was overflowing with all types of suckers, and about half of them were yellow. "You've got quite an obsession with suckers, man. There's like eight shades of yellow in here. Which one?"

"Shut up." He glanced up at Clark to find him laughing silently. "Bright yellow. Those are the lemon ones." Stretching out a hand, he made a come-here motion with his fingers. "Gimme."

"All right, no need for grabby hands." Brian plucked one from the bowl and stripped off the wrapper, then held out the sucker. He grinned when Clark greedily grabbed the stem and shoved the yellow candy into his mouth. "Sweet tooth, huh?" He snorted. "Gotta say, you wrapping those lips around that sucker might be giving me ideas."

"Har har." Clark slotted the candy into the pocket of his cheek, talking around the stem skillfully. "He's a comedian now, folks. Be here all week. Catch a show. Try the veal." Clark leaned over with a sigh, his elbows thudding against the countertop as the animation fled his expression. "I'm tired, Brian. Tired, and I feel grubby as hell. Wanna help me get to the bedroom? I'll grab some things and then tackle that shower we were talking about."

Brian watched as Clark scrubbed a palm over the curve of his head, seeing fatigue warring with pain. And something else. The ease with which he and Clark had settled into this back and forth could have been scary, but he suddenly understood they'd been building up to this for months. *Years, maybe. I know him inside and out, and there's nothing for either of us to fear here.*

"Okay." He closed the drawer and made his way around the island before shoving his shoulder under Clark's arm. "Where we headed?"

"Room past the bathroom. Just need to get some clean clothes." The way Clark stretched before moving said the fall had been harder on him than he might want to admit. Brian preened inside when he realized the man wasn't afraid to lean on him, showing more trust in his actions than could be communicated any other way. "Head's still pounding. Gave myself a hangover, then all that shit on top of it? No wonder I'm tired."

"I've never seen you with more than a beer or two in you. Why'd you get drunk?" He angled them into the bathroom, ignoring Clark's attempts to redirect their progress. "Come in and sit, relax for a minute. I'll grab what you need from your bedroom. Stop fighting me on this."

"Dammit, can't you follow one set of instructions?"

"Apparently not," Brian said flippantly, stepping away from Clark once he'd leaned into the corner where the countertop and wall met. "Why'd you get drunk? You can tell me where to find what you want, or I can go spelunking. Talk loud and fast, old man." He flipped the water in the shower on, then backed into the hallway. "Start soon, or you'll get whatever I find."

"Sweatpants are in the bottom drawer of the dresser, you asshole. Briefs are in the top. Shirts in the middle." Nothing for a couple of breaths, then louder, "Did you hear me, Brian?"

"I heard you. Fuck, you're loud enough. I bet your neighbors heard you too." He opened the top drawer and grabbed the first pair of briefs he saw before closing it. "You that loud for every inside activity?" The bottom drawer stuck, coming to a stop only partway open, and he crouched down to straighten it. As he gave it a yank to unstick it, the drawer exited the dresser, flinging half its contents across his feet. "Shit."

"Shit what?" Hell, he hadn't meant to be so loud, but Clark had clearly heard his exclamation. "Brian, what did you do?"

"Nothing," he singsonged with a grin, staring at what had been revealed in the drawer. Near the back, previously hidden beneath several layers of clothing, were a butt plug and dildo. Stored as they were in the bottom drawer of a piece of furniture all the way across the room from the bed meant the items couldn't be regular play toys. He had a thought and glanced over his shoulder, eyeing the nightstand. Lifting his voice, he called, "Be there in a minute. Why'd you get drunk?" Retrieving a shirt from the middle drawer, he slung the selected clothing over one shoulder, then shoved the mess into the bottom drawer and slid it back into place. Tentatively, with his stomach doing flip-flops, he went to the table next to the bed and opened the drawer. Along a half-empty bottle of lube, there was another dildo, this one larger than the other. "Somebody's vers," he whispered, remembering the feel of Clark's hard dick against his hip the one morning Brian woke in his arms. It had freaked him out so badly he'd slipped away like an embarrassed lover, not even leaving a note on the pillow. Then he'd avoided Clark as much as he could for the rest of the day.

That's what started this shitshow. If I'd just been ballsy enough to stay in bed with him, we might be having a vastly different conversation. Or Clark might not have gotten injured at all. *Because if I hadn't bailed, I'd have been with him.*

"See something you like?" The voice came from the doorway, and he spun, guiltily slamming the nightstand drawer closed behind him. Clark leaned against the doorframe, an uncertain expression on his face, sucker apparently abandoned in the bathroom.

"Yeah." Brian startled himself, his voice coming out rough, ragged, and he sucked in a shuddering breath. "Oh, yeah. I see something I like a fuck of a lot."

"Brian—"

He cut Clark off with a slash of his hand through the air. "Don't. Don't downplay this. Don't rule me out because of my age, or my issues, or whatever awkward arguments you can muster. I was in Kirby's office when you called because I'd decided to talk to him. He was so mad, Clark." Brian hunched his shoulders with a groan. "So mad, and I could see why. From his perspective, I didn't trust him, and when I thought about how it'd make me feel in his place, it was like a knife to the gut." Standing straight, he stared into Clark's eyes, hoping to make the man understand. "I'm tired of hiding. Tired of not being myself, of not feeling like I can be who I am inside. I know..." He shook his head, turning to stare out the window into the backyard. "Like, I-I-I know I did it to myself. Got out, separated, and could have done anything, but old habits die hard."

"They do." He turned back to see Clark hadn't moved, still with one of his broad shoulders propped against the doorframe. "Harder yet when they've been instilled for decades. I get it, Brian. I told you I understand because I do." Clark shook his head in a slow back-and-forth movement, their gazes locked together. "Small towns, military buddies, old friends, family—sometimes it feels like coming out is a forever exercise. Through the years, if I'd had a dollar for every offer to set me up with some nice woman, I'd be a rich man now. But I'm stubborn, and loyal, so even though there was so much pressure, I never caved to it. Never changed who I was inside, even if I was lying on the outside." He held out a hand and Brian crossed the distance between them to slip his palm against Clark's. "I'm tired of pretending too."

Clark lifted his other hand to cup Brian's cheek, and Brian leaned into the touch, the skin against his face hot and welcome and something that made him feel seen. "So let's stop."

"You're so fucking good-looking, Brian."

Without conscious thought, Brian lifted his chin and closed his eyes slowly so that the last thing he saw was Clark's face coming closer.

Hot gusts danced across Brian's skin, accompanied by a whispered, "Makes me crazy to think I could have you."

Then Clark's mouth was on his in a rush of heat, the inflaming touch of tongue against the seam of his lips making him gasp. Clark tasted sugary, like cool lemons, but mixed with a dark bitterness. Brian delved deeper, wanting to chase the bitter away, leaving only the sweetness. It had been so long since he'd kissed anyone, his hookups preferring release over intimacy, but he didn't remember it ever feeling like this. Like he'd go up in flames if Clark stopped. Like the only thing holding him together were the hands cupping his face, fingers tangled in his hair. Surging and then entering a calming lull, the pace seemed dictated by music he couldn't hear, but he went with it, giving up all control to Clark.

Clark owned his mouth, mapping the inside like their lives depended on it. Then, just when Brian was lightheaded from panting and gasping for breath, the man slowed them down, making it clear it wasn't a lack of desire by grinding his hard cock against Brian's. The kiss turned into more of an unhurried savoring, long sips from swollen lips followed by a gentle graze of teeth. Brian buried his face into the fabric covering Clark's chest as they broke the kiss, panting while Clark leaned his forehead against Brian's shoulder.

"Oh, baby. I could kiss you all day long."

Brian laughed softly, breathing deep, dizzy with need as he fed his desire for the scent of Clark. "I'd let you. You've got a talented mouth on you, old man."

"The better to eat you with, my dear." That jolted a true laugh from him, startlingly loud in the quiet bedroom. "Oh, someone likes the sound of that." Clark's hands moved to Brian's waist and hip, the firm grip desperate as Clark ground them together. The heat from Clark's cock branded him even through the two layers of fabric, and he undulated, seeking more pressure until Clark gave a pained gasp.

That was enough to bring Brian to his senses, the sound a bucketful of cold water on his libido.

"Shit, Clark." He shifted away, putting his shoulder back in its accustomed spot. *I didn't even get him into the shower yet.* He was already failing at the tasks set for him by the doctor and Oscar. "You're all bloody still."

"Hey, I washed my hands." The smile aimed his direction held only pleasure and amusement, with no evidence of pain, which made him feel a tiny bit better. "But you took so long, I came to see what the problem was." Clark's mouth turned up a tiny bit more. "I was afraid maybe you'd headed for the hills. You'll never know how glad I am to be wrong."

"I'm sorry." The apology rolled off his tongue effortlessly, something it felt like he did every day. Sorry for his fucked-up head. Sorry for slowing people down.

"Knock that off. If I had worried about you finding something secret, I wouldn't have stayed in the bathroom to begin with." Clark resisted Brian's attempts to turn him back towards the door. "Hey." Head angled down, Brian lifted a shoulder, shaking his head in response. "No, Brian. Look at me, sweetheart." The endearment got Brian's attention, chin lifting automatically as his gaze rose to meet Clark's. "You didn't do anything wrong."

"I was snooping." A bent knuckle under his chin stopped what had become an automatic movement, and he grimaced when forced to keep his gaze on Clark. "That's a shitty thing to do when someone's trusting me."

"Healthy curiosity, I'd call it." Clark's thumb brushed across his bottom lip, and he opened, tongue darting out to

103

try to catch a taste. "Oh, sweetheart." A slow, sly grin fell into place on Clark's face, and when he winked at Brian, the expression turned so sexy he groaned. "We're going to do such wonderful things to each other. But..." Clark shook his head. "Later. Not while I'm still covered in my own blood from the waist down. Not a good look for me." His self-deprecating laughter flowed around Brian, making him smile.

"Okay. Shower, and then we can talk about what I found in your drawer."

"Hopefully we'll have a better conversation about what you find in the shower." Clark grinned crookedly, and Brian surged up to capture it with a kiss that lingered and grew. The softly bemused expression aimed his way after made everything worth it.

"Come on." He nudged Clark towards the door. "Let's get this party started."

"Now you're talking."

In reality, the shower was less sexy and more pain-filled than either of them had expected. Clark drew an involuntary inrush of breath as he lifted his leg to step out of the sweatpants Brian had pulled down. Knowing just that movement hurt Clark certainly made ignoring the gorgeous dick in front of Brian's face just a little easier. *Nothing little about that monster, though.*

He had risen to his feet, steadying Clark while he yanked his shirt over his head. The defiant expression on

Clark's face had done nothing to hide his uncertainty. Brian had rushed to waylay any nervousness by running his hand up Clark's chest, fingers threading through the thick hair there, dark blond strands mixed with the more-than-occasional white.

The muscles underneath were firm, toned in a perfect complement to the rest of his physique. The man might not have a six-pack, but he clearly worked at his conditioning, the broadness of his shoulders offset by a trim waist and slim hips. "I definitely like everything I see here."

Clark's hand had found the back of Brian's neck, drawing him close, pulled up so his face was angled perfectly as Clark's came down.

By the time the shower was finished, though, Clark's expression had been lined and gray. Brian had toweled him off gently, moving quickly to kneel in front of him and reverse the previous process, drawing fresh clothing up to hide the masculine beauty Clark had kept well under wraps.

They'd barely gotten into the bedroom when Brian heard the back door open and close. Clark waved off his concern. "That'll be Oscar. He knows where everything goes. I wanna lie down. I'm tired, Brian."

"I'll bring you some food, soon as I can."

Clark yawned, jaw-crackingly huge. "I'll be very appreciative, I promise. Just slightly delayed."

"Did your drinking set off the back pain?"

Clark shook his head when Brian would have turned back the covers, choosing instead to settle near the top of the bed, back angled against the headboard. "Nah, that's a constant for me. Some days are worse than others. The drinking isn't a frequent thing either. I just wanted a little separation between me and the day."

"Because of me."

The words were scarcely out of his mouth before Clark's hand snapped out and wrapped around his wrist, yanking at Brian so hard he stumbled and half fell onto the bed next to the man. "No, Brian. Not because of you." Clark leaned close, gaze fierce and intense. "Because of all the other people so blinded by their own prejudice that they can't imagine anyone loving inconveniently. Because assholes reinforce the ideas that emotions equal weakness, when telling someone how I feel is the hardest thing I've ever done. Not because of you, sweetheart."

Heat flared everywhere Clark touched him—his wrist, along his thigh, and then the side of his face when a palm grazed his skin there, fingers curling around the back of his neck.

"Never because of you." Clark's mouth pressed against Brian's, and the instant he gasped, Clark licked into his mouth with a groan. Then it was hot and wet and potentially better than the previous kisses. Wrapped up in the still unfamiliar sensation, Brian sank into a dance of lips and tongues that moved together and against each other, until he was again gasping for breath.

A soft knock against the doorframe made Clark pull back, but only a fraction of an inch. Brian opened his eyes to see that intent gaze directed solely on him. "Lie in bed with me?" The question was soft, spoken in a tender tone, and he was nodding before Clark had fully finished speaking. He climbed over Clark's legs, careful of the injured one, and took up a position at his side. Only then did Clark call out, "Come on in, son."

Oscar entered carrying two plates, which confused Brian. The man handed one to Clark and held the other out to him. He took it with a frown and opened his mouth, but Oscar answered before he could even get the question out.

"You'll need to take another dose of meds in about twenty minutes, Brain. It'll be better all-around if you both have something in your stomach." Oscar held out a brown bag, rattling it gently before placing it on the nightstand. "Brain, your pills are in here, along with Uncle Clark's medication from the clubhouse. I figured anything he had here was expired, and when I checked his meds, turns out I was right." Oscar gestured towards the door. "Fridge is stocked, so you don't have to surface for a couple of days if you don't want to." He stretched out his hand, and Clark took it, Brian watching as Oscar bent to brush a kiss against Clark's forehead. "We love you, Uncle Clark, and if you don't take better care of yourself, Kirby's got some ideas."

"Oh, no. We wouldn't want that now, would we?" Clark's voice was filled with wry humor that spoke of ample experience with Kirby's brand of problem-solving, and Brian found he wanted to know everything. *Wanna hear it all.* "Tell your cousin I love him too. You're both real good men, Oscar. Your granddad would be proud."

Clark's smile had changed, taking on a tinge of sadness, and Brian understood in a flash that Clark was the companion Kirby had spoken about. He didn't know what to do with that knowledge, the idea of spending decades being someone's quiet secret, and then he realized he'd been ready to ask Clark to do the same for him. Sickness rolled through his stomach.

"Brain, you with us?"

He looked up at Oscar, seeing a wealth of patience and affection in the man's expression. "What?"

"I asked if you were up to takin' care of Uncle Clark?" Oscar's grin flashed. "He's a handful."

More than that. Brian's brain flashed back to the shower unhelpfully, and he tried to push the memory of undressing Clark to the back of his mind. "Yeah, I got this." Clark turned to look at him, and Brian smiled at the annoyed furrow of his brow and amended the statement. "We got this."

"Okay." Oscar pointed a long finger in his direction. "Meds." The finger turned to Clark. "Fucking take care of yourself." He ambled towards the door, pausing before he went through the opening. "And Brian, get your head out of your ass, yeah?" Then he was gone, the back door opening and closing in the distance.

"Pull my head outta my—? What the hell?" Heat settled high on his thigh, and he looked down to see Clark's hand resting there. Turning, he found a broad grin on that mouth he'd just been kissing and leaned closer as if drawn to the man. "What are you smilin' at?"

"Love those boys like they're my own. It was a thing of pride when they started callin' me Uncle Clark. That faded as they grew up, and I became just Clark through time. Their grandfather died—Pops, or Dall, as I called him. They went to war and I stayed here. Never expected to see them again. I wasn't family, you know?"

"But you are." Brian didn't understand where this story was going but felt compelled to offer the truth as he saw it. "They love you."

"Yeah. And I'm proud of that fact. But when Kirby came to town spouting these grand ideas of changing the club, the thing I saw as Dall's legacy, I was pissed as hell at that boy. Gave him a real hard time." The fingers on his leg squeezed, and Brian covered Clark's hand with his own. "I get it now. Hell, I got it within sittin' through a couple of his passionate lectures about the old guard not being what the new generation of veterans needed. I could see it in his struggles and in the way that Oscar's service changed him." Snorting a laugh, Clark shook his head.

"You young bucks came through the door, and I slowly got to know each of you. Took me only a little time to understand how the club, Kirby's foundation, was what you *had* to have to regain things war took from you. Just like

Dall had understood when he founded the club decades ago that our generation needed to know we weren't alone. That's the basis behind every major club founded after World War II or Vietnam. Gave us a circle of brothers who'd been there, who'd seen what we'd seen, done the things we were forced to do. Similar, but different from what's needed now. Hell, there's so much that I understand now but didn't in the beginning." Clark cleared his throat and settled the plate in his lap, staring down. "And then, those boys picked up callin' me 'Uncle' again, like a badge of honor, and I felt it *deep*. I'm proud of them, proud of what they're building, and pleased about being part of that."

"Why do I feel like there's a 'but' in here somewhere?" Brian tucked his fingers underneath Clark's palm, liking the bright hum in his chest when his hand was gripped firmly in response.

"But I'm tired of hiding half of who I am. If Kirby and Oscar can deal with me and my history in their family—" Clark shook his head side to side slowly, his gaze fixed on the sandwich "—which hasn't always been easy, then the rest of the brothers should be able to manage, right?" Brian's fingers tightened around Clark's hand, and he caught the flash of a smile that lightened his expression for a moment. "Those same fears you have, I carry every single one of them. Still, if you're lookin' for someone to burst free alongside you and take half the heat, that could be me. I love who I love, and my service to the club stands outside of that."

"*I love who I love*" buzzed through Brian's head. Those words could have been generic, but deep down, he knew they weren't. Something told him that Clark had spoken from the heart. Brian fumbled with his plate, resting it onto his lap like Clark's before he reached over to turn the man's face towards him. A deep frown pulled Clark's brows together, and Brian smoothed over the lines with his thumb until they eased. *Am I gonna do this?* "I love you too." Words he'd never spoken to another man fell out of his mouth, and his breath caught on a sudden intake.

Clark's features softened, laugh lines crinkling his cheeks and the corners of his eyes as he smiled wide, that damned crooked tooth peeking out. "Yeah?"

"Oh, yeah. If love is getting a stupid grin on my face every time I think about you, which is a lot. Or feelin' like a whole flock of something's taken up residence in my chest when you walk in a room, then yeah, I love you." Dragging his fingers along the side of Clark's face, he traced the outline of the man's mouth with a fingertip. "You sat down beside me on that damned couch, called me names, and dissed my games, and that caught my attention. I was crushing on you hard. I never expected—" He shook his head. "Finding you at the bar was like a lightbulb went off in my head. I knew you hadn't freaked out with my handsy ass in your bed but never thought there'd be a chance for me."

"Oh, baby, we're going to talk about those nights soon. But right now, I really want to kiss you." Clark leaned closer. "Then, if my leg and back allow, I want to fill that ass and fuck you hard. Are you up for that?" Clark's voice had dropped an octave, the rough edges scraping along every nerve Brian had, lighting him up from the inside out. "Fuck you, take you to the edge and push you over. I have dreams about that ass, boy, and I'm dying to know if I can make them all come true."

The kiss started slow, an easy coming together as if it were something they'd done for years. Nothing about the caress was tentative or cautious. Clark owned his mouth exactly as Brian had hoped for—biting and licking, teasing touches of his tongue. They led to Brian's following until Clark suckled hard, a promise of other activities Brian would be entirely on board for. But later. Right now, their connection was everything, and when Clark eased backwards, Brian chased his mouth, earning himself a renewal of the kiss until they were both breathless.

"Sweetheart," Clark murmured against his lips. "Slow, slow. Waited for this long, you and me can wait a little longer. Slow, sweets. We've got all night."

Brian pulled back, staring into eyes that seemed to only see him. "All night." His throat and chest got tight. "Storms tonight. I don't know." He tried to clear his throat, but the thing choking him refused to be dislodged. "I don't know what that'll mean."

"Means you need to eat your food, and so do I." Clark dropped a tiny pecking kiss at each corner of Brian's mouth. "Eat, sweetheart. I'm not going anywhere."

Ten minutes of near silence ended with both plates empty, and Brian slipped out of bed. He held out his hand wordlessly and accepted Clark's dish, piling it on top of his. After walking to the kitchen, he rinsed both plates and placed them in the empty dishwasher.

Glancing around the house, he picked up on more details this time through. Glimpsing a picture of a younger Clark piqued his interest, and he ambled into the living room, pausing in front of the fireplace. In pride of place was a triangle holding a folded American flag. The plaque affixed to the wooden frame was engraved with Randall Mayhan and dates that were likely the club founder's birth and death. Right above that was a rectangular shadowbox with a thick row of medals and ribbons and a bronze tag in one corner saying they'd been awarded to Clark Donaldson. Brian studied both items, one a reminder of Clark's longtime lover and one commemorating a service the man didn't like speaking about.

"Kirby and Oscar did both of those."

Brian turned to see Clark in nearly the same pose he'd been earlier, this time against the corner of the archway leading from the kitchen to the living room.

"Week after Dall's funeral, the flag showed up, and my service box went missing. A few days later, the medal display was up there. It's got my paperwork tucked inside the back, including the presidential pardon for the crime of lying about my age. They did their research; everything's in the right place, just where I'd have pinned them on my dress blues."

The photo just to the side of the flag recaptured Brian's attention. Pops, a figure well known from all the pictures at the clubhouse, stood next to Clark. Taken probably twenty years ago, the photo showed a respectable foot of distance between the two men. "This is you and him. That's the clubhouse."

"Yeah. That's Dall." Clark's voice was as rigid as the figures in the picture, and Brian turned to look at him. Emotion twisted his face, something between anger and grief. "We always had an annual memorial ride for his wife. That was the ten-year run." *Ten years and they'd been together for at least half of those, and they still couldn't touch.*

"Let's go back to bed." Pacing towards Clark, Brian extended his hand, relieved when it was clasped in return. Arm around Clark's waist, Brian led the older man to the bedroom, wondering at the incongruity of their shifted roles. Releasing his grip at the foot of the bed, he paused, ready to take his cues from Clark. Surprising him, the man started the process of undressing, making a sound of frustration when the sweatpants tangled around his ankles. Brian quickly stripped and went to his knees, gratified when Clark's hand rested on his shoulder. He took the other man's weight as they straightened things out, leaving Clark naked. Brian rose to his feet and steadied Clark around to one side of the bed, then backed onto the mattress, flipping the covers back in invitation. "Come on, Clark. Lay with me."

Clark sat and retrieved the bag Oscar had brought over, removing the containers and studying the labels. "Here's yours." He popped the cap and shook two tablets into his hand, dropping them into Brian's palm a moment later. By the time Brian had finished swallowing them, Clark had taken his own medication and returned both bottles to the bag on the nightstand. Sliding to his back on the mattress, he groaned soft and low, a sound that caught at Brian's chest. "Feels good to stretch out."

"Yeah." Brian eased closer to Clark, enough to be within easy reach. "You got a good bed."

"Better now you're in it." Clark's gaze met Brian's and held. "You ready to hear what I want?"

"Maybe?" Brian cleared his throat. "Um. Probably."

"Well, don't sound so enthused. Gonna give an old man a complex." Lines creased in the corners of Clark's eyes when he smiled. "Seriously. We've shared some information and know more about the other, but I don't want there to be any confusion or gray area about where I stand. Probably better to put it out there and see if we're on the same page."

Under the covers, a hand clasped Brian's and tugged, pulling harder until he shifted closer to Clark. He came to rest plastered against the man's side, leg propped across

Clark's uninjured thigh, where stiff hair prickled his skin. "I'm listening."

"Good. Listen, and really hear me, Brian. Really and truly hear me." The inrush of air swelling Clark's chest had Brian breathing deep in a sympathetic response. "I want to be with you. In bed, of course. That goes without saying, but maybe shouldn't. I want to do dirty, filthy things to you, things that you'll remember for the rest of your life, because we'll repeat all the ones worth doing again. Over and over. Practice makes perfect." Another deep, heaving breath caught in the middle so that Clark's voice started out soft and airy. "I want to stand with you and be with you, regardless of where we are or who's there to see. Arms around your body, chin on your shoulder, mouth on your neck—and not give a shit about anything except making you smile and laugh. I'm tired of hiding what I feel, sweetheart. Tired of digging deep for love I've had to bury when right now, all I have to do is reach out and grab hold. I want that. I want *you*. More than you probably know." Clark's hand covered Brian's chest, fingers coming to rest over his heart. "I want to know I've got you. Need to believe that there is an *us* in all this."

"How can I make you understand you've already got all that? Right here, Clark. I'm right here, man." Brian tipped his head back, focusing in on Clark's blue eyes. *Prettiest color in the world.* "I'm not going to promise it won't be without hiccups, because old habits die hard. But I can promise you that I'll do my damnedest to be worthy of you. I'll work hard. You can bet on that."

"You already are worthy, you little asshole." A dark chuckle filled the air between them, mattress shaking lightly with Clark's laughter. "I'm just too damn old to pretend anymore." Fingers threaded through Brian's hair, tightening and tugging enough to sting. "But I'll take the promise in the way it was meant, as a declaration."

Clark turned to face Brian and skated a hand along his ribs. By the time the caress got to the crease of his groin, Brian's dick was entirely on board with the idea, rigid and standing out from his belly. "Shit, all you gotta do is breathe my direction and I get hard."

"Yeah?" Fingertips danced a circle on his hipbone and then traced a trail across sensitive skin. "How hard, sweetheart?"

"So fuckin' hard." He bit down on his lip, trying to hold in the sounds that wanted to escape. "Jesus, Clark." Nails scratched through the pubes surrounding the root of his dick, and he held his breath. "Please. Oh, please."

"This?" Fingers wrapped around the base of Brian's cock, and his hips thrust, erection tunneling through the loose grip. He keened as he shifted towards Clark, chin lifting in response to the yank against his hair. "This what you want, sweets?" Hot breath touched his lips, and he lapped at the air, groaning when Clark's mouth covered his, the palm and fingers now moving with a casual regularity along his dick, stroking in rhythm with the tongue tangling with his. "Oh, Brian."

The pressure on his dick disappeared, and he cried out into Clark's mouth, frustrated and needy. So fucking needy, he didn't know what to do with the feeling, the urgent demand of his body to be closer to this man. "Lick," Clark demanded, and Brian stuck his tongue out, painting Clark's palm with saliva. A finger dipped across his lips, and he pulled it inside, suckling hard, not complaining when it thrust in and out, never quite disappearing. "God, boy. The things you do." Then the finger was gone, replaced by Clark's tongue.

The slickened palm wrapped around him again, with the addition of Clark's rigid erection. Steel covered by soft skin, and the scent of precum filled the air as Clark thrust, his movements cautious. Fingers jacking up and down his length paired with the feel of Clark's dick sliding through the slick provided by his own spit was nearly enough to push him over the edge right then. The ridge of his cockhead caught and pushed against Brian's, creating a different cadence of weight and release that had him rushing towards the finish line far faster than he wanted.

Clark broke their kiss, panting as he planted his forehead against Brian's. Brian opened his eyes to find Clark staring at him, face flushed, lips parted as he gasped for air. "You gonna come, sweets?"

Brian nodded, picking up the rhythm and fucking into the tight fist when Clark paused, holding still.

"Yeah, boy. Take what you need from me. Tell me what you want and I'll do it. I'll fuckin' do it, sweets."

"Just like that." His hips stuttered at the pleasure twisting Clark's features. "You touching me like this?" Gasping in a breath. "So good. Better than I imagined."

"Come on, Brian. Come for me. Want to feel it and see you." Clark's hips moved again, the push and pull too much.

"Oh, God." Balls tight to his body, he didn't try to hold back, giving way and letting the electric rush that had been building in his belly expand to fill every inch of his conscious mind. Hair prickling with gooseflesh, he clutched at Clark's arm, at the back of his neck, at the covers over them and let his head rock backwards, losing himself in the sensation. Heat covered his dick. "*God.*"

"Yeah." Clark's thrusting sped up, his hand working to pull the last splashes of hot liquid from Brian's overworked dick. *He's using my spunk to jack off.* That shouldn't have been as hot as it was, but Brian's brain wasn't engaged in that moment. "Now, sweets." More heat covered his dick, the smell of Clark's orgasm another shot in the gut, and Brian's dick gave a half-hearted twitch before he pulled his hips away.

"Too much." He didn't resist as Clark's grip in his hair pulled and twisted, tucking his face into the crook of Clark's neck. He breathed deep, taking in that scent he'd come to associate with this man. Heart still pounding fast, he sucked in another hard hit of that smell, burrowing closer. "God."

"Nope, just Clark." The lame joke made him chuckle, and when Clark joined him, the rattle and shake of his amusement transferred through Brian's entire body.

Settling into the mattress, he smiled when he heard Clark give a loud yawn. "Can't be assed to clean up. Fucked me stupid, sweets. That's a good thing."

"I'll get a cloth in a minute."

"I won't be awake in a minute." Clark's breathing changed, and Brian tensed, waiting. "You gonna be here when I wake up?"

Oh, God. The hurt he'd delivered days ago reared up and smacked him in the chest.

"Yeah. Gonna need a crowbar to pry me away from you now, old man."

"Good thing I don't own one, then." Clark's arms tightened, his hand soothing the back of Brian's skull and neck, holding him close. "I like you here, Brian. And that's God's own truth."

"I'm staying." He pulled in a breath. "Promise."

Tension fled from Clark's frame, and he sighed heavily. Then his head dropped to the pillow. "I believe you, sweets." Brian rolled sideways and stood up. "Where you goin'?"

"Clean you up. You can't sleep with a handful of spunk without getting it everywhere."

By the time Brian returned from the bathroom with a warm, wet cloth, Clark was already sleeping.

Boocoo Dinky Dau

He lay there with a soft smile, the edge of his crooked eyetooth peeking out from between his curved lips.

Chapter Twelve
Old Boots

Staring, he took in what the bathroom mirror was telling him.

In the three weeks since Brian had installed himself into Clark's home, his features, hell, the entire makeup of his countenance had changed. Gone were the dark circles under his eyes, the heavy scowl, and what had become his constant resting bitch face.

In their place were laugh lines at the corners of his eyes, and even the newly growing scruff attempting to be a beard couldn't hide the all-the-time upturn of his lips. Kirby had commented on the changes last night, turning the whole thing into a dirty joke—just like he would have done with any of the club members. Clark had been standing behind Brian, arms loosely crossed over his man's chest, when Kirby started spouting nonsense. The instant tension in Brian's muscles had slowly bled away as Kirby continued, giving them harmless grief echoed by input and laughter from the other members.

Then Clark had taken Brian home, put him in the bed he'd been calling "theirs" in his head, and fucked him into the mattress after a tantalizing session of teasing foreplay.

"Down, boy," he muttered, glancing down at his cock, which had attempted to rise at the memory.

That was another thing. He might not have the refractory period of his twenty-year-old self, but then again—*This me is having a hella lot more sex than twenty-year-old me, so it balances out.* And sex with Brian was never boring. The man had a pent-up imagination, and Clark found a deep desire to see every wish Brian had brought to fruition.

Hence the date today.

"Brian, get your ass up and movin'." Clark grinned at himself in the mirror when he heard Brian's grumbled argument from under the pillow he likely had pulled over his head. *That man's an avoider if he can manage it.* "There's a turnout up in the Queen that's got our name on it."

A few days ago, Brian had talked in detail about a desire to have semi-public sex. Got him so turned on that Clark had scarcely gotten him prepped that night, sliding his cock in slowly to the chorus of Brian's groans about coming too soon. *Might need to invest in a cock ring.* Clark's grin widened. *Not that Brian complained about the second orgasm I forced from him.*

"Where we going again?" Brian stumbled into the brightly lit bathroom, eyes half closed as he moved unerringly to Clark's side. This assurance of a warm welcome was relatively new, a demonstrated confidence following Clark's constant reinforcements that he was ready to be as open as Brian wanted in their relationship. "And why do we have to start so early?"

"Queen Wilhelmina State Park. It's about three hours straight up into Arkansas. Wanna get there early enough to grab lunch. Then we'll head west into Oklahoma." He rubbed his cheek against the top of Brian's head, whiskers catching on the tousled hair. "Be a good day for a mountain ride."

"You said something about a turnout?" Brian's reflection smiled small, the soft curve of his lips inviting.

"And me on my knees, sweets." At Clark's gruffly growled words, Brian's eyes shot open, muscles tensing all through his body. "If you're so inclined."

"Oh, I'm inclined." Brian arched backwards and stared up for long enough that Clark dipped his head to capture those tempting lips in a hard close-mouthed kiss.

"So am I." He pulled back and stared into Brian's eyes, losing himself in the depths. "You know I'm keeping you, right? From here until eternity, I'm making you mine."

Making a statement like that should have been frightening and wasn't something he'd have dared to say to Dall. *I also didn't feel like this with Dall.* True thoughts, because while he'd grown to love Dall, the emotions were all tied up with honoring the sense that Dall had saved him. Brian was saving him in a different way, breathing new life into an old existence and forcing Clark to reevaluate his own wants and needs. "I don't know what I'd do without you, Brian. Being with you makes everything...different. *Better.* Like I'm only half breathing when we're not together."

Brian's expression slowly morphed from the pleased softness suffusing his features post-kiss into a more serious look. Not scowling or angry, but intent in that way which made Clark feel seen. Measured and weighed, and he could only hope he wouldn't be found wanting.

"Keeping you, too, old man. I hope you don't have any ideas about leavin' me in your dust." Clark shook his head vigorously, and Brian grinned fleetingly. "You know the prognosis for my TBI, and it doesn't seem to scare you."

"No, baby. I also know that things change, and nothing is guaranteed. Hell, even pleasure rides like today come with risk. For once, I'd rather not focus on the potential storm on the horizon and pay close attention to what's right in front of me." He tightened his arms around Brian, pulling him close. "We both need saving sometimes, and I'll always be that for you."

"Back atcha, old man. I'll always be here for you, as long as it's in my ability to do so. I'll fight for you." Brian tipped his forehead forwards, connecting with Clark's chest, and Clark kissed the crown of his lover's head. "Fight for us. You and me, we're worth the effort."

"We so are, sweets. We so are."

~~~

THANK YOU

Thank you so much for reading *Boocoo Dinky Dau*, book four in my Mayhan Bucklers MC series. These stories have a dear place in my heart, and I hope you've enjoyed them all.

ABOUT THE AUTHOR

Raised in the south, *Wall Street Journal* & *USA TODAY* bestselling author MariaLisa learned about the magic of books at an early age. Every summer, she would spend hours in the local library, devouring books of every genre. Self-described as a book-a-holic, she says "I've always loved to read, but then I discovered writing, and found I adored that, too. For reading...if nothing else is available, I've been known to read the back of the cereal box."

Want sneak peeks into what she's working on, or to chat with other readers about her books? Join the Facebook group! **bit.ly/deMora-FB-group**

deMora's got a spam-free newsletter list she'd love to have you join, too: **bit.ly/mldemora-newsletter**

~~~~~

ADDITIONAL SERIES AND BOOKS

Please note that books in a series frequently feature characters from additional books within that series. If series books are read out of order, readers will twig to spoilers for the other books, so going back to read the skipped titles won't have the same angsty reveals.

Rebel Wayfarers MC series

A motorcycle club can be a frightening place, filled with hardened men and bad attitudes. Rebel Wayfarers is a club with their own measure of hard and dangerous, led by their national president, Davis Mason. This book series follows members as they move through their lives, filled with anguish and heartache, laughter and love. In the club, each of them find a home and family they thought long lost to them.

Mica, #1
A Sweet & Merry Christmas, #1.5
Slate, #2
Bear, #3
Jase, #4
Gunny, #5
Mason, #6
Hoss, #7
Harddrive Holidays, #7.5
Duck, #8
Biker Chick Campout, #8.5
Watcher, #9
A Kiss to Keep You, #9.25

Gun Totin' Annie, #9.5
Secret Santa, #9.75
Bones, #10
Gunny's Pups, #10.25
Not Even A Mouse, #10.75
Fury, #11
Christmas Doings, #11.25
Gypsy's Lady includes *Never Settle*
        (#10.5), #11.5
Cassie, #12
Road Runner's Ride, #12.5

Occupy Yourself band series

Stardom doesn't happen overnight. Hell, it doesn't even happen after a decade in the business, as the members of Occupy Yourself have found out. But, with the right talent and the right representation, they might still have a chance to make it big. As long as they can keep their lead singer sober, keep their drummer focused on the music, keep their guitarist out of trouble … well, you get the idea. Come and join us, stand side stage for a close-up view of the backstage happenings in a rock-and-roll band. It's guaranteed to be a show you won't ever forget.

Born Into Trouble, #1
Grace In Motion, #2 (TBD)
What They Say, #3 (TBD)

Neither This, Nor That MC series

Legends are born from moments like these. Folktales spun around a single point in time so perfect, you can almost hear the click resonating through the universe as things align. Meet Twisted, Po'Boy, Wrench, Retro, and Ragman, good old boys from southern states who have many things in common. First, is a bone-deep love of the biker lifestyle. Second, would be their love of the brotherhood, and knowing that you trust the man at your back. Finally, these men have the love of a good woman. None of these come without a price, and it is our pleasure to journey along with them as they discover the blessings that can be won, and lost along the way.

Rebel Wayfarers crossover stories

Enjoy these stories that tie the different worlds of my MC universe together, bringing Rebel Wayfarers MC and the clubs of the Neither This Nor That series into glorious alignment.

> *Going Down Easy*
> *No Man's Land*
> *In Search of Solace*

Mayhan Bucklers MC series

The Mayhan Bucklers MC has been part of the rolling hills of Northeast Texas for decades. Now, new life is being breathed into this reborn club, a legacy resurrected by grandsons of the founder. The MBMC is set to surpass its original glory, fortified with an honorable purpose: Helping wounded warriors reintegrate back into society, gifting those who've given so much with a safe place to land.

Learning how to navigate life while war still echoes inside you isn't easy, but with solid brothers at your back anything is possible.

> *Most Rikki-Tik*, #1
> *Mad Minute*, #2
> *Pucker Factor,* #3
> *Boocoo Dinky Dau,* #4

Borderline Freaks MC series

When you can't count on anyone else to save you, there's only one real choice. Borderline Freaks MC is a series of books about the men of the club and their brotherhood — and of course the love they have for their women. Take a trip along with Monk, Blade, Wolf, and Neptune, and feel for yourself the connection these men have for each other.

Service and Sacrifice, #1
More Than Enough, #2
Lack of In-between, #3
See You in Valhalla, #4

Alace Sweets series

Dark romantic thrillers, these books are not light reads. Filled with edge-of-your-seat suspense, intense stories command the reader's attention as they drive towards their explosive endings. Alace Sweets is a vigilante serial killer, with everything that implies and is sure to trip all your triggers. Be ready.

Alace Sweets, #1
Seeking Worthy Pursuits, #2
Embarrassment of Monsters, #3
All the Broken Rules, #4 (TBD)

With My Whole Heart series

Sweet as pie and twice as delicious, these romantic love stories are a guaranteed happily-ever-after read.

With My Whole Heart, #1
Bet On Us, #2

If You Could Change One Thing:
Tangled Fates Stories

When threads in the tapestry of life are cut short, inexorably changing the future for those you love, would you be willing to tempt fate to set things right?

> *There Are Limits*, #1
> *Rules Are Rules*, #2
> *The Gray Zone*, #3

Other Books:

> *Hard Focus*
> *Dirty Bitches MC: Season 3*

~~~~~

deMora's Rebel Wayfarers MC and the Neither This Nor That MC series do cross over, along with the Occupy Yourself band books, so readers have a couple of choices. The series can be read independently beginning with RWMC, OYBS, and then NTNT without too many spoilers. There's also a crossover between deMora's RWMC world and Lila Rose's Hawks MC world. Or they can be read intertwined—in chronological order.

Here's the recommended reading order if you want to follow according to timing:

Mica, RWMC #1
A Sweet & Merry Christmas, RWMC #1.5
Slate, RWMC #2
Bear, RWMC #3
Born Into Trouble, OYBS #1
Jase, RWMC #4
Gunny, RWMC #5
Mason, RWMC #6
Hoss, RWMC #7
This Is the Route of Twisted Pain, NTNT #1
Harddrive Holidays, RWMC #7.5
Duck, RWMC #8
Biker Chick Campout, RWMC #8.5
Watcher, RWMC #9
Treading the Traitor's Path: Out Bad, NTNT #2
Living Without, Lila Rose's Hawks MC:
	Caroline Springs #4
Shelter My Heart, NTNT #3
A Kiss to Keep You, RWMC #9.25
Gun Totin' Annie, RWMC #9.5
Secret Santa, RWMC #9.75
Trapped by Fate on Reckless Roads, NTNT #4

More information available at **mldemora.com**.